W9-DIW-361

STORIES TOLD BY THE AZTECS

Before the Spaniards Came

STORIES TOLD BY THE AZTECS

Before the Spaniards Came

CARLETON BEALS

illustrated by Charles Pickard

Abelard–Schuman

London · New York · Toronto

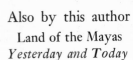

Also by this author
Land of the Mayas
Yesterday and Today

London	*New York*	*Toronto*
Abelard-Schuman	Abelard-Schuman	Abelard-Schuman
Limited	Limited	Canada Limited
8 King St. WC2	257 Park Ave. S.	1680 Midland Ave.

Printed in the United States of America

23950

Contents

Introduction

The Aztecs of Mexico were good papermakers and recorded their history on parchment in hieroglyphics and
colored pictures known as codices. Spanish conquerors
wished to wipe out the Aztec religion and Aztec ideas and
memories in order to impose the Catholic religion and Spanish rule. The few codices that have survived are mostly now
in museums in the Vatican, Madrid, Paris, London, Berlin
and Dresden. From these and other sources it has been possible to retell some of the original pre-Spanish legends.

As in present-day comic strips, the narrators are shown
with lariats of words coming out of their mouths. They are
shown in their bright clothes, their low-cut blouses (*hui-
piles*), their skirts (*cueitl*). They are shown talking, praying
to the gods, preparing their food in glazed terra-cotta ware,
grinding their corn on the *metatl*, a slanted three-legged
stone; weaving their cloth, doing inlaid featherwork, carv-
ing their musical instruments and dart-throwers (*atlatl*) and
polishing their precious stones. Doctors or medicine men
and women cured sickness with herbs and incantations.

They used anesthetics long before Europeans did; they filled teeth and did trepanning—boring a hole in the skull to relieve pressure on the brain.

The codices show the Aztec warriors, the Knights of the Eagle, the Knights of the Jaguar, going to battle, fighting. Their merchants crossed the mountains over trails lined with agaves, or century plants. In this picture-writing the Aztecs told of their work, their way of life, their legends, history, religion and philosophy.

The greatest collector of codices was Lord Edward King Kinsborough, who spent his life and his money trying to prove that the Aztecs were Egyptians.

A few of their stories were written down by early Spaniards, a few in the original Aztec. Such Aztec and Spanish chronicles preserved legends old and new, the poetry, the noble epic of Quetzalcoatl, the verses of Nezahualcoyotl, the drum songs, the spring songs and the harvest songs. Out of them emerges the picture of a phenomenal culture. Father Bernardino de Sahagún lived among the Aztecs and observed their mode of life. He noted their religious rites and heard their legends, and wrote them all down in Aztec in twelve volumes that he translated into Spanish twenty years later.

Some of their stories are older than the Aztecs—told by pottery shards and charcoal and skeletal records that date back 12,000 years or more, to the age of the great mastodons. But the Aztec learned the older legends and added them to their own collection.

Such records tell of the early migrations of the peoples. Mostly they cluster around three gods. (1) Quetzalcoatl, the Plumed Serpent, who drove out earlier animal gods and

led the Toltecs in the Central Valley of Mexico; (2) Tezcatlipoca, the Black Mirror that Smokes, leader of the Chichimeca or Stone Men; (3) and Huitzilopochtli, the Left-
legged Hummingbird, the Aztec war god, also known as
Mexitli, Heart of the Maguey, after whom modern Mexico
is named. The successive supremacy of these three major
gods indicates, if only vaguely, prehistoric migrations into
Anahuac. For the Aztecs accepted and venerated the gods
of all their predecessors, but their greatest god was the
Humming Bird, who guided them into the great Valley of
Lakes.

Originally a skeleton, he was reborn full-armed—shield
and spear, green-plumed helmet and serpent girdle of precious stones—from a bunch of bright feathers under the
embroidered tunic or *huipil* of Serpent Skirt, Goddess of
Spring.

Near the huge carved war god in the National Museum of
Mexico stands the colossal figure of Coatlicue, his virgin
mother, a fearful mass of writhing serpents and skulls, the
epitome of terror.

The codices also tell of the destruction of the four suns,
the heavens and the mainland, and the creation of the Fifth
Sun, under which mankind now lives. The men under this
sun were made from the Bone of the Dead, which the
Plumed Serpent stole from Mictlán, the Mansion of the
Dead. On his way back to earth he was attacked by quail,
emissaries of the Lord of Death. He fell down and splintered
the bone into pieces—which explains why men are of different height and girth.

There are 4,000,000 Aztecs living in Mexico today who
speak the language of their ancestors. It is one of the most

beautiful and melodious of languages—sweeter but stronger than Italian, softer and less emphatic than Spanish. One writer has called it "the language of nightingales." The Aztecs still tell stories of the ancient days, of the old gods, the battles of the past and the life of their forefathers. They are a living part of Mexico. They are Mexicans.

❀ ❀ ❀ ❀ ❀ ❀ ❀ ❀ ❀

CHAPTER 1

The Valley of Mexico

The Valley of Mexico, more than 7,000 feet above sea level, is set among lofty mountains that are sometimes snow-covered. In Aztec days it had five enormous lakes and was called Anáhuac, meaning "land on the edge of the water." Being so high, it was mostly free from the insects that plague man and his crops, and the strong ultraviolet rays from the sun killed many germs quickly, thus reducing sickness. Fruits and flowers tumbled forth abundantly, and enormous cypress trees as large as the California Sequoias, or redwoods, rose majestically from the rich soil. Many, originally planted by Emperor Moctezuma in the royal gardens at Chapultépec (Grasshopper) Hill, still grow there, magnificent with long misty veils of gray-white Spanish moss.

The Aztecs grew maize, or corn (said to have been given to them by the Plumed Serpent), of many colors—yellow, white, brown, red, blue, green. They cultivated many kinds of beans, numerous varieties of squash and pumpkins, calabashes, gourds and sweet potatoes. Mostly their hot chile, for seasoning, and their many fruits were brought in from the hot country. Over the upland valley stretched farflung fields of maguey, the agave or century plant, looking like monstrous artichokes.

That growth was a jack-of-all-trades. The fibers shredded from the long fleshy leaves were used to make rope and twine, nets to bind together crates and furniture and bags, mats and tapestries. The sap was medicinal, containing nearly all the vitamins, and today it is canned and used in the United States for certain ailments.

Left to ferment, it provided a frothy milklike beer that was often flavored with strawberries, cherries, plums, pineapples or zapotes. The sharp, hard thorns were used as pins and needles, and during wartime shortages they were imported into the United States as phonograph needles. They were also used to prick ear lobes, fingers or arms to extract blood for religious penance.

The first people came to Anáhuac 16,000 years ago, according to the system known as carbon-dating. About 12,000 years ago a hunter chased a mastodon into a swamp and drove a spear into his flank. Both left their bones there. Some 7,000 years later, half a dozen varieties of food crops were being grown in the valley.

The final wave of peoples to this region, several thousand years ago, was made up of Nahuatl, of which the Aztecs were the last invaders. The first were probably the Toltecs, —The Builders, or first pyramid people. The Aztecs from the northwest arrived after wandering homeless and harassed over the upland plateau for hundreds of years, before building their great city in the Texcocan marshes and becoming rulers of a vast empire.

Around 1040 they had set forth ten thousand strong from

their seven caves in the twisted hill on lovely Aztlán Isle, "the White Land," eternally carpeted with the snow of heron feathers. The word of their god rang in their ears: "I shall free you . . . and march with you." He promised them fertile lands and wealth, robes of rich plumage, precious stones and beautiful women, an Eden of "goodness, tranquility, fragrance, flowers, tobacco, music . . . everything you wish, whatever you may desire. . . .

"You shall go conquering, you shall go defeating. . . . You shall go spreading terror—*Tlacatecó Tonauautilli*, 'The Magic of Blackness!' All captives are to be offered up on the stone of sacrifice; you will slice their breasts with the quartz knife; you will offer their hearts, likewise their blood to the Moving Sun, that it may continue to shine clearly; you will eat of their flesh. . . ."

Finally the Aztecs fought for a foothold in that lofty Anáhuac paradise. For long years they were enslaved, then they fought free. Obeying the instructions of their War God. Huitzilopochtli, the Left-legged Hummingbird, they founded a settlement deep in a Texcoco Lake swamp where an eagle with a serpent in his beak perched on a nopal cactus. That was in 1324 or 1325.

A difficult and unlikely place! They had to build their thatched huts on stilts and make artificial milpas, or fields, on which to plant their crops. However, there were birds and fish galore and the Aztecs had always been fisherfolk. The swamp provided such delicacies as salamanders and frogs and marsh-fly roe. And there were many flowers, just as their god had promised. The tiny settlement of thatched huts on poles grew into mighty Tenochtitlán, with a quarter-million people. Beautiful palaces, temples and pyramids rose along its canals. This too, the god had promised, a splendid city-to-be, mother of a hundred other cities.

Some centuries later, the Spanish conquistadores could not conceal their amazement at this vast metropolis that was larger and more magnificent than any in Spain. In November, 1519—in the Aztec Month of Flags, of military displays, when all prisoners were required to make impressions of their hands in wet cement—the conquistador Hernán Cortés stood in his incised Toledan armor beside Emperor Moctezuma (clad in jeweled feather robes, turquoise bracelets and gem-incrusted gold-soled sandals) on the five-story ramparts of the central pyramid, or teocalli, the "God House," and looked across the serpent-walled quadrangle over the temples and palaces and glistening white-coated homes.

In the main market, or *tiánguiz*, it was reported by Bernal Díaz, one of Cortés' soldiers, there were never fewer than 40,000 people. On that shimmering morning, in the dry season, the flat roofs were alive with people brought out by the beating of the great temple drums; the canal streets were swarming with thousands of flower-decked canoes and brigantines with awnings of painted reed. Lighthouses on city walls guided fishermen. Great dykes kept out the lake floods. Three cement-paved stone causeways, eight pasos, or nearly fifty feet wide, with towers, gates and drawbridges, radiated out for miles, north, west and south across the lake. The mighty mountains were freshly decked with snow and the valley was crowded with a score of cities on the shores of the five lakes. Some of these wonders Cortés described in his *Letters to the King*.

To the southeast ran a chain of lower truncated cones.

Closer to the city Cortés observed a smaller eminence, the Big Rock, the Peñón, active with bubbling hotsprings. *In 1803, three centuries later, the German scientist Alexander von Humboldt prophesied that someday the Peñón would inundate the city with molten lava.* The Aztecs had their own legends of doom; the eventual destruction of the Fifth Sun—the one we now live under. *Four previous suns, they believed, had been obliterated in earlier catastrophes. So every century the Aztec priests held elaborate fire ceremonies to stave off the anticipated disaster.*

Directly across Lake Texcoco there shone in Cortés eyes the houses and temples of Texcoco, an older, more cultured center, founded in 1115 by Xolotl (deified as the magical Double God), reputedly a twin of Quetzalcoatl, the powerful white, yellow-bearded Plumed Serpent. Here was maintained a fine arts academy for poetry, musical composition and dancing.

Some years before the Spanish Conquest, Texcoco had been ruled by the poet-king Nezahualcoyotl (Hungry Coyote), a great astronomer and promoter of arts and crafts. Some of his nostalgic philosophical verse has come down to us; several couplets are engraved over arches in the modern Education Building.

"These glories (of the Great Ones who have sat upon Thrones) have passed like the dark thrown out by the fires of Popocatépetl, leaving no monuments except the rude parchments on which they are recorded."

At the head of a large bay, that November morning, Cortés could see the serpent pyramid of Tenayuca, built by Xolotl's people, rebuilt by the Aztecs. At the end of the north causeway, arose the sacred Tepeyac (Nose of the

Hill) with its shrine, or *cu*, for Tonantzín, Our Mother, the popular Earth Goddess. *In due time it would be replaced by the venerated Christian shrine of the miraculous Virgin of Guadalupe, with blue sky and golden stars about her shoulders. This shrine has always been a place of healing, first for the Aztecs and later for Mexican Catholics.*

Cortés was impressed by the royal summer palace—the temple, fortress and hunting lodge of Chapultépec—rising above the giant *ahuehuetl* cypresses. From Chapultépec and nearby Coyoacán, The Dog Town, at the edge of the lava flow, aqueducts of double terracotta pipes on brick arches brought fresh water to the one-time swamp city. *The Spaniards foolishly destroyed them and for nearly fifty years had to have water brought in by carriers. Much of the city's modern water supply still comes from the abundant Chapultépec fountains, which figure in the ancient legends of emperors and princesses.*

Far to the southeast, Cortés saw the lofty saddle of snow that his little army had crossed between towering White Popocatépetl (Smoke Mountain) and Ixtaccíhuatl (White Woman). But his eye could not reach to the limits of the empire, stretching far north and deep into Central America.

The Aztec capital, Tenochtitlán, after its heroic founder-chief Tenoch, was called The Center of the World, also The Stone Place of the Heart of the Maguey. Its mighty square, three times the size of the plaza of Salamanca in Spain, was alive with a hundred smoking shrines. It contained dance squares, the Priest House (Calmecac), schools for girls and boys and for the training of warriors. *Even today, though reduced in size and renamed the Zócalo (Moorish for "Base of the Edifice") the square is one of the world's largest civic plazas.*

It was dominated by the grandiose teocalli with its great staircase and by the Imperial Palace, which covered the equivalent of four large modern city blocks. The Palace housed barracks, harem quarters and steam baths. Its zoological gardens contained specimens of every bird and animal, even rattlesnakes, and had ponds for wading birds such as scarlet flamingos.

"It sounded like hell," said Bernal Diáz, "when all the tigers [jaguars] and lions were roaring, the jackals and foxes howling, the serpents hissing." There were concert and dance salons, a library of picture codices, laundries, kitchens and numerous banquet rooms.

The Emperor, the Spaniards reported, ate from a gold-inlaid table, with tablecloth and napkins, and had his choice of thirty courses—stews, meats, pheasant, sweets and an incredible assortment of fruits. He was served by four beautiful girls and attended by four nobles who ate, standing up, whatever the Emperor deigned to hand them from his plate. The meal was enlivened by buffoons, dancers, singers and musicians.

The endless reception rooms were full of gold and stone statuary. The walls were sheathed with carved-stone slabs, sheets of gold, parchment and leather tapestries, frescoes, cloth and feather brocades, and with emeralds, jade and turquoises. The first loot, hastily collected by the Spaniards —and largely lost when they were driven out—was valued at millions.

The palace, built of hewn blocks of rose-colored *tezontle* lava, was roofed with cedar. *The blocks were later reused in the National Palace, the main staircase of which is now adorned with Diego Rivera frescoes in a style reminiscent of pre-Conquest art. Aztec stone blocks, from buildings destroyed by the Spaniards, were also used for the other rose-colored arcaded Spanish buildings that encircle the plaza.*

On the south side of the Imperial Palace was the Volador market and fair grounds, with stalls of leatherwork, hand-woven textiles, feather inlays, jewelry, paintings, carved canes and painted gourds.

The Volador grounds had a court for *tlachtli* (the throwing), a combination of basketball and soccer, over which the grinning Opatzín, the Monkey God, presided. The hard ball, made of rubber—a miraculous substance unknown to the Spaniards till they landed in Cuba—could not be touched by the hands, but had to be driven by feet, arms, heads or bodies through vertical stone rings, encrusted with jade and jewels, that were set at each end of the court. *One pre-Spanish legend tells how two rival emperor-gods settled their right to rule by a tlachtli game; how the loser surrendered all his temples, palaces and concubines and departed from the land—a genial way of determining political succession.*

In the volador, another sport, there was a tall pole topped with a revolving platform from which participants, dressed as bright birds and attached to multicolored ropes, launched themselves into space. They soared round and round until finally they came to rest at the base of the pole. The ceremony, costumes and crisscross pattern were a reproduction of the sacred Aztec calendar, a Sun-Moon-Venus affair.

In the Aztec Empire was embedded the semi-independent Tarascan capital Tzintzuntzán (Hummingbird Place) on Lake Pátzcuaro (Place of Delights). Also encircled by the empire was the fiercely independent "Kingdom" of Tlaxcala, which had withstood a salt blockade for more than a century. Salt, at that time, was as crucial for empire building as oil wells and uranium are today.

Beyond the confines of the empire, many peoples—some in what is now the United States—paid tribute to the Aztec Emperor. Some twenty southeastern Zapotec towns made payments of gold, jade beads, quetzal feathers, cochineal dyes and textiles. Gold was also imported from Panama. Such was the Aztec Empire by the time the Spaniards came. *The legends that follow were told by the Aztecs or by other peoples from whom the Aztecs adopted them hundreds, even thousands, of years before the conquest.*

❀ ❀ ❀ ❀ ❀ ❀ ❀ ❀ ❀

CHAPTER 2

A Universe Is Born

In the beginning was Ometecutli,[1] Lord of Duality, so called because he was both male and female. He was night and day, life and death, therefore the fountainhead of creation, the source of all life. From him came all.

He was the Supreme Being of the Aztecs, The Lord of All Creation, He for Whom We Live, He Who Has All Within Himself. He existed before the Heavens came into being, before Earth swung on its axis, before Man was known, before the Land of the Dead was fashioned, before the abodes of the Hereafter were shaped. He is pictured with the Aztec symbol of light on his brow, to indicate that his wisdom was all-powerful and that he had within himself the Creative Fire.

For fire was the first thing created by the Lord of Duality—fire and light. And since fire is "creator of all," so the god first created himself. Thus fire and the supreme being are one and the same thing—immortal and everlasting fire and light, the fire that gives life, the light that leads light.

[1] See page 198.

Next, the god proceeded to create thirteen heavens.[2]

The two upper heavens, Omeyocán, Double-Place, were for the supreme god himself. Sometimes he divided his functions, and his consort was known as Omecíhuatl, Woman of Duality, symbolized in Aztec painting by a nose ornament in the form of a temple upside down.

The heavens beneath were destined for lesser gods still to be created. Immediately below, the Lord of Duality fashioned the Heaven of the Red God, a red mansion for the God of Fire-to-Be, that is, fire in the physical earthly and astral sense, not the universal creative fire embracing all attributes that Ometecutli himself represented.

Beneath this, he shaped the Heaven of the Yellow God, the golden mansion for the God of the Sun-to-Be. In it were also to dwell many other gods and goddesses, also the deified warriors killed in battle and the deified mothers perishing in childbirth.

Next, the Lord of Duality made the Heaven of the White God, the white mansion of the Evening-Star-to-Be: the Plumed Serpent.

To shroud these superholy mansions in mystery and conceal them from the direct gaze of man, Ometecutli created an intervening dark heaven, the Heaven of Storms, the Heaven of the Moon, since the moon—a place of intense cold raked by furious tempests—caused the earthly storms that were so disastrous to the corn crops. In this dark heaven, the God of the Dead was to rule.

The Lord of Duality also created the lesser heavens, called Ilhuicatl. First, the Blue Heaven, the actual sky or firmament we see during the day, was created. Below, the

2 See page 199.

Lord of Duality laid out the Greenish Black or Dark Heaven, the Heaven of Night, sometimes called the Ball-Game-of-Stars. Then came the Heaven of Comets—the Stars-that-Throw-Arrows, the Citlamina, which bring disease, death and war upon mankind. In fact, it was a comet that brought the dread tidings of the coming of the Spaniards and the overthrow of the Empire.

Still closer to earth came the Heaven of the South, the dwelling of the Goddess of Salt. It was a secondary abode also for the White God of the White Heaven, the twilight place where this god would be directly visible to man as the Evening Star. Next came the heavens in which the Sun, or Yellow God, the Blond-God-of-the-Golden-Rays, was actually to be seen from the earth. Next were created the Heavens of Stars and Rain and of Air and Clouds, where Moon shone.

Finally, the Lord of Duality created Earth, but left it unfinished and unpopulated, a task to be completed by the lesser gods. Last of all, he laid out the Road of the Dead over which the souls of the dead would have to pass in order to reach their final destiny.

One day in eternity, the Lord of Duality created the divine pair: Tonacatecutli and Tonacacíhuatl, the Lord and Mistress of the Fruits of the Field, of Life and Sustenance. Tonacatecutli was the symbol of the Sun; Tonacacíhuatl was the symbol of the Earth. From the union of the two sprang all fertility.

In Aztec painting, the Lord of Life always appeared with his body painted black with holy rubber sap and adorned with stars. Behind his head was the outspread fan of the God of the Dead. In his right hand, he held a gigantic eye beneath which was a star shining in the center of a sun—the ensemble signifying Light from Above. In his left hand, he held a yellow vase containing many ears of corn, sustenance for mankind. His consort also carried corn—in her ear, or as loose grains or as meal or dough: *nixtamal*—ready for consumption.

This divine pair had four sons: Xiutecutli, the Yellow God of Fire; Tezcatlipoca, the Black, the Dark-Mirror-that-Smokes; Quetzalcoatl, the Plumed Serpent; and Huitzilopochtli, the Left-legged Hummingbird.

The God of Fire was the source of the visible fire of the earth, the fire of the altars and the fire of volcanoes.

Smoky Mirror, the Moon, was present in all parts and in all hearts; he knew all thoughts and everything every man did. He was the God of Magic, of eternal youth, of music and the dance, and of eternal love and romance.

The Plumed Serpent was white, the Evening Star. He was also Air and Wind and the Cleaner-of-the-Rain-Roads. It was he who set the first moon in motion with a single breath.

The Hummingbird, the terrible God of War, at first born a skeleton, possessed no precise color. Later, he was reborn a full-sized warrior, clad in blue and completely armed and ready for battle.

The gods did not do anything more for eleven Aztec "century" cycles: 572 years. The world was slowly being born. But one day, all the gods got together and decided to complete creation. They created the Goddess Chalchuitlicue, Skirt-of-Green-Jade, or Emerald Skirt, to preside over the newly made waters on earth. Into these waters, they put the griffin-crocodile man-fish called Cipactli. His ridged back "turned into the continents"—a poetic way of saying they emerged from the depths of the sea.

He was the Night. His wife, Oxomoco, was Mistress of the Day. To him the gods gave orders to till the soil. His wife's duties were to sew and weave. Both were patrons of the magical and mundane arts. They helped discover corn, the meaning of time, and the calendar and they were advisers during the early Toltec and Chichimec migrations.

Their offspring was Piltzintcecutli, the Young Lord. He was seated on a throne, his arms outstretched. Under his eagle-headed helmet, the upper half of his red-bearded face was yellow, with a square, dark-red patch under each eye. From his necklace was suspended a human heart, and in his mouth was a circular object symbolizing birth. He was present at all childbirths.

The gods made a woman for him out of two hairs from the Goddess of Love, Xochiquétzal or Flower Feather. Thus was the earth populated. Men of that first race were giants, the Quimametzín.

The four main gods, observing how little light the Evening Star gave, decided to make a sun. Smoky Mirror was given the honor. He ousted the White God—the Plumed Snake, the Morning Star—from dominance in the skies and thereafter shone as the principal body of light.

❀ ❀ ❀ ❀ ❀ ❀ ❀ ❀ ❀

CHAPTER 3

The Four
Destructions of Mankind

The first Sun created by the gods, the Sun of the Smoky Mirror—*The Four Jaguar Sun*—Nahui Ocelotl, shone on the world for centuries until the Plumed Snake, still angry at having been displaced, gave the Black God a tremendous beating and hurled him headlong into the sea.

The Black God turned himself into a jaguar and saved himself by swimming to shore. By then he was so hungry that he flung himself upon mankind and devoured it, giants and all.

To record this happening, the Black God became a constellation in the form of a jaguar, "The Great Bear." It appears to sink each night into the sea as though actually falling from heaven.

This first solar catastrophe occurred at the beginning of the fourth Jaguar century, exactly 624 years after that sun began to shine. It took another fifty-two-year cycle to eat all mankind, so that in all the reign of the Four Jaguar Sun lasted 676 years, or thirteen Aztec centuries.

New men were created, and the Plumed Snake remained

as Lord of the Sky, the Four-Wind Sun—Nahui Ehecatl. But the old feud went on, and the Black God eventually knocked him out of the sky again. The fall of the Plumed Snake, who was also the Wind, caused such a terrible hurricane that the whole earth was devastated, and men were changed into monkeys. This era lasted seven Aztec centuries, or exactly 364 years.

The Black God gave the job to Tlaloc, Wine of Earth, God of Rain—The Four-Rain Sun, Nahui Quiauitli. After 312 years, or six Aztec centuries, the Plumed Serpent, still jealous, caused fire and lava to rain from heaven. Tlaloc was dethroned. To escape, the third race of human beings turned into birds.

In Tlaloc's place, the Plumed Serpent put Chalchiutlicue, Emerald Skirt, the Goddess of Water, the Four-Water Sun —Nahui Atl. After thirteen Aztec centuries or 676 years, her reign ended with a catastrophic flood that covered the whole world, causing the fourth race of men to turn into fishes, except one pair who were warned to embark in a hollow cypress tree.

When the tree finally touched ground the couple cried out, anguished in the darkness, to the Citlaltonac, Stars-that-Don't-Shine, the Stars of the Milky Way, and to their consort, Citlalicue, Star-Skirt, also of the Milky Way. The couple cried out: "Who makes light? Who illuminates the world?"

This so infuriated the gods that Smoky Mirror rushed down to earth and angrily "cut off their necks at the bases" and replaced their heads with the heads of dogs, and "dogs they became."

In the Vatican Codice, an ancient Aztec manuscript preserved in Rome, the story of the four Suns is told in more detail, but in different order. The first destruction was by Water.

Disgusted with mankind, the gods charged Emerald Skirt, Goddess of Water, to punish them.

Emerald Skirt was beautiful. Her lovely hair was crowned with a blue diadem, banded with red and surrounded with waving green plumes. Her earrings were turquoise. About her neck a gold medallion hung from a collar of precious stones. Her blouse and her skirt were banded with wave-like blue, like a lake rippled by the wind. On her swift feet were white open sandals adorned with red bows.

Her eyes shone with terrible brilliance. Seizing a banner, on whose folds were depicted the symbols of rain, storm and lightning, she hurled herself through space and planted it upon the summit of a high mountain. Immediately menacing clouds gathered.

She went down to the valley and entered a small house where lived an honorable married couple, makers of the beverage called pulque. The man was named Coxcox (Pheasant) and the woman was called Xochiquétzal (Precious-Flower-Feather). The man and the woman gazed upon their beautiful visitor in admiration.

To them, Emerald Skirt apparently said: "Make no more pulque. Look up at that mountain; from there will come a great flood that will overwhelm the earth. Cut down this hollow *ahuehuetl* and get inside it. Take with you the fire from your hearth. Each of you must eat only one ear of corn a day."

Hastening back to the cloud-crowned mountain, she looked sternly in the four cardinal directions, then waved her banner with both hands and all her strength. Lightning flashed, thunder crackled, cataracts fell from the sky. Rain and hail pounded the earth and mighty torrents swept over everything—fields, towns and cities.

The terrorized people sought salvation in trees and on the hills. Weeping, they begged for mercy. "Oh gods, let us become fish!"

"Fish you shall be," responded the gods, according to one account, and the people, as they sank into the raging flood, turned into fish.

But the privileged couple floated safely in the trunk of the holy *ahuehuetl*. Their charcoal hearth-fire sparkled cheerfully.

The waters finally subsided. The earth dried out, and just when the survivors had finished their last ear of corn, their improvised boat grounded on the side of Mount Culhuacán, the sacred hill of the gods. With great reverence, they carried their precious fire to their new home. The gods instantly provided them with food, and the couple gave thanks to divine providence.

They were blessed with many children, but all were dumb, till finally a bird taught them various languages.

Mankind lived under the Air Sun (*Ehectonatiu*), but again aroused the wrath of the gods. Quetzalcoatl, Plumed Serpent, God of Air, was charged with carrying out the decree of destruction.

The Plumed Serpent was white, but his face and body were painted black with holy rubber sap. His jaguar-skin miter was adorned with green quetzal feathers; he wore huge earrings of turquoise and a collar of gold, from which

hung large snail-shells, symbolizing the wind. The yellow, red and green plumage, streaming like a long cape over his shoulders, resembled fire. In his right hand he carried a serpent staff; in his left, a red shield on which was the white wind jewel.

He approached a thatched cabin where a man and his wife were tranquilly talking. Peering through the cane stalks, the god looked upon the loveliest creature ever seen. From her sleeveless embroidered blouse, her copper shoulders and arms emerged full and round; her legs, showing through the front slit of her hip-wound skirt, were slim and strong. Her glossy black hair was dotted with white flowers. She was certainly worth saving.

Sharp gusts of wind came through the walls from the panting of the god. He entered between the cane stalks.

"Listen to me carefully," he whispered melodiously. "Take your hearth fire and hide yourself in a cave in the nearby mountain." He was the beneficent wind from the east, from the garden of paradise, but soon, he warned he would blow from the north and from the south as a furious hurricane and sweep over the entire world.

He flew up into the clouds where his servitors, the four Winds, bowed reverently, and he gave orders for them to blow toward the earth with all their might!

The four servitors opened their unusual mouths, puffed out their elastic cheeks and let loose a puff toward each of the four cardinal points. They grew more ardent, until their blowing became a hurricane. Whirlwinds and cyclones swept over the world, picking up sand, stones, rocks, waters and finally trees, houses and human beings. The snowy capes of the mountain peaks were whisked away, converting the whole world with an immense white sheet.

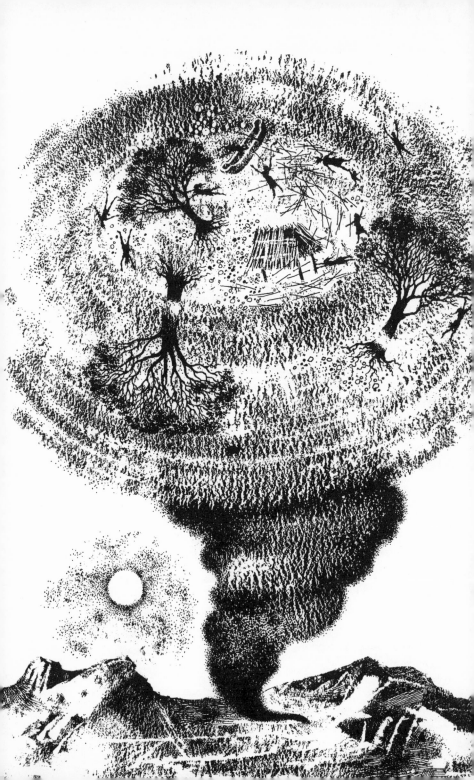

Nowhere could the panic-stricken humans find safety. If only they were animals they could escape. The gods turned them into monkeys.

As monkeys, they fled in fright through the mountain ravines.

The chosen man and woman, in their cave beside their red hearth fire continued their conversation, unperturbed by the roar of the wind, not feeling the glacial cold that gripped the world.

THE FIRE SUN (TLETONATIU) ruled in the sky for centuries. Once more the gods, displeased with mankind, called upon Yellow Face, Xiutecutli, God of Fire, to carry out their decree of destruction.

The Fire God, with his fierce face and frightful protruding teeth, wore a parchment crown of various colors with flame-like plumage. He was nude, except for slippers with rattles. Putting aside his war shield, he caught up a bunch of yellow feathers—a handful of lightning bolts.

In a village beside a tranquil fire, a married couple talked of their many hopes. Suddenly the fire crackled, and from the end of a cane stalk, burning with a pure blue flame, came a heavy voice that seemed to say, "O privileged mortals, talk no longer. Do you not hear a deafening, subterranean sound underneath your feet? That boiling fire will break through the crust of the earth. Get up at once, take the fire from your hearth to a cave in the woods."

Obeying the god's mandate, they hurried into the woods with their hearthfire and some household utensils. Hardly had they found a refuge, than the earth shook and the mountains rocked in gigantic convulsions. From the crater of the nearby volcano leapt a menacing figure—the God of Fire. On his back floated his cape of lightning bolts. From a box producing deafening explosions, he dumped out red hot stones. Fire and lava whirled down.

The volcano vomited heavenwards a stream of vapor, shot through with lightning, lighting the whole earth with a livid yellow glare. Cinders and burning sand rained down. Plants were reduced to cinders, trees were snuffed to ash, stones melted. Flaming lava swept down over the woods, the plains, fields and houses. Men and women were suffocated, their flesh and bones melted away.

"Ah, if we were only birds, we could fly away!" they exclaimed.

The gods turned them into birds.

As birds, they flew about blindly, emitting pitiful cries.

But there in the center of the woods, in the fold of a hill, in a great cave, hidden by the foliage of the trees, the chosen couple conversed peacefully beside their hearth fire.

UNDER THE EARTH SUN (TLATONATIU)

The human species multiplied and was evil, though many people were good. This time the gods decided to destroy only the wicked and called upon Chicomecóatl, Seven Serpents, Goddess of Earth, to carry out the decree.

Seven Serpents was young and beautiful. Save for two white bands, her dress was solid red from head to foot. She wore glistening pendants and a collar of golden ears of corn. Her sceptre was two fat ears of red corn with golden tassels—symbols of her sway over the fertility of the fields.

Smilingly she gave orders to the Gods of Fire, of Water and of Air, her friends and collaborators. As Sterility and Hunger, she now denied her fruits to mankind.

No rain fell. The fountains ceased to flow. The fields

turned to drifting dust. Despair rose from one end of the land to the other. "Have mercy!" cried the people. "End our hunger and our thirst!"

From time to time Seven Serpents sent a little water—but only to the good people.

"Save us!" the wicked ones kept crying, but the jaguars, also starving, ate them up. Apparently anguish-stricken by such misery, Seven Serpents ceased acting as the Goddess of Sterility and Hunger, and became Chalchiucíhuatl, the Emerald Woman, the Goddess of Fertility and Fruits, of Abundance. She became Xochiquétzal. Precious Flower Feather and wife of God of Corn. She called on her collaborators to give rain and warmth to the earth.

The streams rushed gaily over the dry, hot sand. Earth turned green again. Trees blossomed. The surviving people planted every sort of seed; corn and beans and chili. Soon the cultivated fields were bright with verdure. Soon the granaries were bursting with grain.

These various destructions of the world mirrored race memories of early catastrophes that wiped out whole peoples—floods, hurricanes, earthquakes and volcanic eruptions. Perhaps one of these myths reflects the great downpour of fire and lava that long ago swept away the folk of the circular wind temple of Cuicuilco in the southern end of the Valley of Mexico—so swift and terrible it even left embracing skeletons for future anthropologists to uncover and measure.

❄ ❄ ❄ ❄ ❄ ❄ ❄ ❄ ❄

CHAPTER 4

The
Fifth Sun

After the last destruction, the sky fell upon the earth.
Alarmed at such a cataclysm, the four main gods opened
four roads underneath the earth and created four strong
giants to help them. The Smoky Mirror and the Plumed
Snake converted themselves into colossal trees with powerful trunks. The giants, the trees, the other gods, all lifting
together from underneath, replaced the sky just as it had
been before.

Overjoyed, the Black God and the Plumed Serpent raced
across the sky in swift chariots, leaving in their wake in the
blue sphere a path of sparks—the Milky Way, the Cloud
Snake called Mixcoatl.

After the fourth sun fell in flames on the High-Rock-of-
the-Gods, the world remained in utter darkness, with no
dawn, no day, no twilight. The gods, perhaps bored by
their own laziness, decided to give the world a fifth sun.

They assembled at Teótihuacán, Place-of-the-Gods, the
holy city. *Even before the Aztecs, it was a great center of
Toltec culture.* They must make both a Sun and a Moon,

they decided. One of them must change into a Sun, another into a Moon. Who was best suited?

Tlaloc, Earth-Wind, Lord of Rain, suggested one of his own four hundred assistants, known as Tlaloque—Little Rain Lords. The Tlaloque selected was Napantecutli, Four Quartz, Four Times a Lord. His special duty was to provide rains for the matmakers so reeds would grow fat and strong.

But Tecuciztécatl, the Lord of Snails, a rich and noble god, spoke up, saying he was quite willing to change himself into the Sun.

No one else volunteered. Among them was a poverty-stricken girl with a spotted face, who smiled when they looked at her. She was Nanahuaztzín, Poor Leper. Little Boils, they called her, because her body was covered with sores. Though only a demigoddess, she lived in beautiful Tamoanchán, the privileged abode of the Eagle and the Jaguar, of the Hawk and Wolf, the heaven of the Seven Winds and Seven Flowers.

They decided she would be the second one to bring light. She protested that she was a little sick person, not truly a goddess. They promised to restore her to health by giving her their own blood and healthy complexions.

Preparations were made for the ceremony. Two enormous pyramids, with wide stone staircases, were erected; one was for the Sun, the smaller one for the Moon. On top were constructed altars in which the Sun god and the Moon goddess were to be worshiped. The two chosen did proper penance, pricking themselves with maguey thorns and with obsidian knives until they bled. Both gave offerings. Those of Lord Snails were rich; those of Little Boils were modest.

He offered fine sprays of leaves and flowers, rich gems and emerald green feathers; instead of the usual balls of straw, balls of pure gold; instead of maguey thorns, thorns of rose-colored coral. Poor Little Boils could not offer even flowers, only green canes, tied three and three, and five little balls of straw, and maguey thorns stained with her own blood.

They bathed. Little Boils had no fine clothes to put on, so she varnished her ulcered body white and put on a thin torn paper dress, through which her body showed. The Lord of Snails put on fine feathers and precious flowers, luxurious robes and sparkling jewels.

The noble Lord of Snails paced about, shivering with cold and fear, biting his lips and spitting frequently. Little Boils, the humble one, sat quietly, her hands crossed in her lap, smiling happily.

The gods lined them up on either side of a great fire, and gave instructions. To become the Sun, the Lord of Snails had to throw himself into the heart of the fire.

He turned pale. Three times he tried to throw himself into the flames, but lost his courage.

The gods told humble Little Boils to try it. Smiling sweetly, she closed her eyes and without hesitation threw herself into the heart of the flames.

Ashamed of himself, the noble god gathered all his courage, but again hesitated before his final leap and fell upon the glowing cinders and turned to ash.

An eagle swooped down, passed squarely through the flames, singeing the tips of his feathers so that they became coarse and black. A jaguar followed. His fur was scorched with permanent black and brown spots. Came next a hawk, whose feathers were charred coal black. Then a wolf, who got toasted, but only to an ash color.

Suddenly, the flames parted and two luminous balls came forth, one in the beak of the eagle, the other in the claws of the jaguar. The regal bird sailed majestically off and deposited the golden ball in the gate of the East. The jaguar raced off, crossing valleys and mountains, and placed the other luminary beside the first.

Little Boils, having jumped full into the flames, was far brighter, and so became the Sun. The cowardly Lord of Snails was dimmer and became the moon.

There in the East, the gods had already constructed a beautiful dwelling for the new Sun. Little Boils was seated on a throne of precious feathers, her lips were painted scarlet, and her hair was lavishly decorated with jewels and fine plumage. She was now the Sun in the dawn crucible of billowing painted clouds; the feathered pearly mist, the green-gold bands of sky. Never was there a dawn more brilliant! The gods were enchanted.

But Little Boils did not move. She just sat there in the East, silent and smiling. For four days she sat.

Why does the Sun not move, the gods asked, and Little Boils reminded them that they had promised her their clean blood and beautiful complexions, their high rank.

Tlalhuitzcalpán-Tecutli, God of Twilight-and-of-the-Ice, God also of the Evening Star, set a long arrow, shanked with feathers of all the colors of sunset, and let fly. But he was so angry that every arrow went wild.

Little Boils, still smiling sweetly, drew forth one of her own arrows, shanked with bright sun-colored feathers, and shot back, then started after him.

He fled through all the nine nether heavens. She followed close behind him through the same heavens and passed out of sight in the west—the eternal drama of the Sun pursuing the Evening Star.

But some say that the God of Ice-and-Twilight was the Plumed Serpent, and that his arrows were wind arrows. He blew with such force that both heavenly bodies started through the sky, the Sun in front, the Moon after.

One of the gods, watching the spectacle, since the Sun took so long moving, hungrily devoured the offerings he had brought. Then as the Sun moved upon its course, frantically he seized up everything that came to his hands, the rocks, the sticks, but threw them aside as unfit for offerings. As the Sun sank in the west, he grasped at the very shadows lengthening over the earth and was lost in them. He was still empty-handed. The Sun punished the god's negligence by converting him into the Buzzard, *Huinaxcatl*, Mere-Bone-and-Feathers, and condemned him for ever after to seek among vain shadows, hungry, never satisfied.

The gods, according to this version, told Papachtoc—Medicine Straw, God of Drunkenness, to get the Moon moving. Seizing a rabbit, symbol of drunkenness, by the hind legs he struck the Moon full in the face. Ever since, the Moon has retained the deep scar of this blow—the long ears and flying legs of a rabbit.

Reluctantly, the Moon also started to move. At the crossroads of the sky, the Tzitzimiman, the Lightning Spirits, Goddesses of the Flowing Tresses, who holds up the sky, and the Coleletín, the Air Spirits, pointed after the Sun, indicating the road she was to follow.

And so he followed Little Boils, but when he got to the

far west, the Sun had long since set. By then the body of the noble Lord was covered only with rags that scarcely concealed his nakedness.

CHAPTER 5

Plumed Serpent

For centuries Quetzalcoatl, the Plumed Serpent, was the major god of the Toltecs. Later in Tenochtitlán, he had one of the major temples in the great central square. It was snow-white and round, symbolic of the whirlwind—the only circular edifice there. A White God, he had come from over the seas and taught the people new handicrafts and to grow better and different crops.

He was finally driven back over the sea by Smoky Mirror, who ruled the high temples of the Chichimec invaders. Then, after many centuries, the Hummingbird, the Aztec War God, came to hold the leading role in Aztec temple ritual. Actually the Plumed Serpent remained the favorite, most potent god of the people. He had brought peace and prosperity. And so, whatever the religious preferences of the nobles, warriors and priests, the Plumed Serpent always remained more beloved.

Some day, it was believed, he would come back from over the sea to restore the golden age and once more teach his humble followers the wiser ways of plenty and peace.

Shortly before the arrival of the Spaniards, omens and por-
tents spread the word that the second coming of the White
God was at hand. Mexican people were psychologically
conditioned by this "second coming of Christ" to submit
to the conquerors. Cortés inherited the mantle of the
Plumed Serpent.

The name "Quetzalcoatl" is derived from *coatl*, snake,
and *quétzal*, the beautiful green bird of Chiapas and Guatemala. The delicate plumage of the quétzal was the symbol
of the wind, of water and of fire. An enormous plume of
quétzal feathers flowed down the god's back like a green
tide.

His face and body were usually dyed black with rubber
sap, with painted red stripes, and his lips were vermilion.
His eyes, heavily circled with black, typified the night sky.
His hook-shaped ear pendants were turquoise, and from
his gold collar hung little snailshells. His turquoise snake
mask, inlaid with jade, gems and gold, was snouted to represent the wind. His mitre was of black-spotted jaguar skin,
sometimes red-dyed leather, with a top-knot of quétzal feathers. His short skirt was embroidered and his short trousers,
held by a red sash, were of jaguar's skin, adorned with
small snails. His sandals and leggings were black or white
with red bows. In his right hand he carried a red shield,
white-bordered and decorated with the jeweled sign of the
four-pointed wind. His staff, encrusted with precious
stones, was shaped like a question mark.[3]

The Mexicans called the wind *ehecatl*, shown hiero-
glyphically as a fantastic head with a long snout, and

[3] See page 199.

Ehecatl, the Plumed Serpent, always wore his wind mask and a spiral shell representing eddies of the wind. Since the wind god induced sleep and helped conceal unusual noises, thieves always carried an image of the Plumed Serpent. All his words were auguries. The rustle of leaves and stalks, the sighs from the trees, the wailings of the tempest, the hollow sounds through the narrow openings in the rocks, the swish of air through cracks in the walls—all were messages that holy men could interpret.

Thus the Plumed Serpent was Ruler of the Air. With a breath he could create round temples. He ordered the breezes or the tempests to blow from whatsoever direction. The gentle balmy wind of the East came from the Sun paradise, Tlalocán; that of the North came from the infernal region, Mictlán, and was furious. The cold wind from the West came from the Sun habitation of deified mothers, the Cihuapipiltín. That of the South, from the realm of Huitznacóa, Goddess of Salt, was often boisterous, sometimes of hurricane force, tearing out trees and throwing up huge waves that destroyed vessels.

Peasants invoked the god at the first breaking of the soil, asking for strength to work the earth. Woodsmen begged the god to protect them against falling boulders and trees or cutting themselves. The Spanish chronicler Pedro Ponce relates how woodcutters, before entering the forest, prayed to the Plumed Snake, asking his permission to cut the wood, telling him it was not out of lack of respect. They promised the god that the cut wood would be venerated by all men.

The woodsmen made notches in the middle and at both ends of a felled tree trunk, into which they put tobacco, or *picietl*, then struck a few blows on it with a pole, and once more asked the Plumed Serpent to help them to drag it into the village so no one would be injured by the heavy timber. When large stones had to be transported, much the same procedure was followed. Most loads, before being transported, were smoke-darkened by burning copal in honor of the god.

The Plumed Serpent was also the Evening Star and the Morning Star. The Pacific Coast Nahuatl saw the Evening Star float for some time on the sea before vanishing into the waves. Its light, reflected in the moving swells, was like a brilliant snake. In fiestas the alchemists mimicked the astronomical phases of the Evening Star. The processions and dancers approached his temple through arches decorated with flowers, rich feathers, birds and rabbits. First came a person with boils, a clownlike personification of the Sun, who complained bitterly of his affliction, but interlarded his whining with witty sayings. Next came two blind persons —Clowns of Darkness. Clowns of Twilight followed, eyes bleary with twilight cold and drunkenness. The blind joked with the bleary-eyed.

A person apparently suffering from a cold in the lungs came wheezing and coughing and jesting about his infirmity. He was the Clown of the Wheezing Evening Wind. A large fly buzzed furiously—the insect drone of twilight. Finally a beetle, rolling his eyes, came searching for offal.

The temple of the Plumed Snake, called Ilhuicatitlán, On-the-Heavens, was often erected above a tall pyramid with a majestic staircase flanked by gigantic carved stone snake heads. The feathered coils and long undulating horizontal tail clasped the pyramid in their embrace. His temple also had a large court with a theatre thirty feet square. It was always whitewashed and profusely decorated with branches and colored paper.

❋ ❋ ❋ ❋ ❋ ❋ ❋ ❋ ❋

CHAPTER 6

The
Four Hundred Nebulae

The parents of the Plumed Serpent were Mixcoatl, the Cloud Snake, the Misty Serpent, *i.e.*, the Milky Way, and beautiful Shining-Shield-in-Hand, a clever agile girl.

Skirt-of-Fine-White-Stones had given birth to the Cent-zón Mimizcóa, four hundred stellar deities, the nebulae of the Milky Way. *They were, perhaps, the invading Stone Men from the north.*

Skirt-of-Fine-White-Stones led her four hundred prog-eny into a large cave with seven grottoes, the star caves, the caves of lightning and comets. There she gave birth to quin-tuplets—Mixcoatl, Misty Snake; Cuautlicóatl, Eagle Snake; Cuetlaccíhuatl, She-Wolf; Tletepetl, Mountain Hawk; and Apantecutli, Lord of Irrigation Canals.

The Four Hundred were jealous, and the Quintuplets, to escape, went into the water where they remained four days. They were weaned on honey water, the sap of the maguey and on pulque, the wine of the maguey.

So ugly were the Four Hundred that Skirt-of-Fine-White-Stones gave the quintuplets to Mexitli, Navel of the

Maguey, Lord of the Earth, to nurse and raise. *Not yet identified with the Aztec War God, he was still an Earth God of fertility.*

The Four Hundred were wastrels. They dressed themselves in gay raiment, got drunk on pulque and caroused. Earth Lord gave them shields and arrows and told them to go hunt for their food. The weapons were adorned with precious quétzal plumes, with the plumes of the white heron, the divine red flamingo, and the Blue Bird. Earth Lord taught them to make more arrows and how to use them in the hunt and in battle. But the Four Hundred merely amused themselves foolishly, shooting only small birds. They gained the derisive nickname of "Bird-Shooters." On several occasions they did kill a jaguar, but made no offering to the Sun. They would not let the quintuplets come back even to visit the seven caves.

Exasperated, the Earth Lord armed the quintuplets with maguey thorn darts, gave them his sacred shield, and told them to go destroy the worthless Four Hundred northerners.

The five hid themselves in the crown of a mesquite tree. Who is hiding up there? the Four Hundred demanded.

Eagle Snake hastened to conceal himself in the heart of the tree trunk; Misty Snake went into the earth; Mountain Hawk went into the heart of the mountain; the Lord of Irrigation ducked into the water. She-Wolf bounced a rubber ball to hide her intentions. The Four Hundred were perplexed that the five had disappeared.

The wood of the trunk split apart with a roar, and the branches cracked about the heads of the Four Hundred. Eagle Snake burst forth. The earth shook as Misty Snake writhed forth. The mountain burst asunder and tumbled down in a mighty avalanche. The Mountain Hawk whirled down. The waters boiled as the Lord of the Canal leapt forth. She-Wolf tossed aside her ball and raced to join them. They defeated the Four Hundred. All but half a dozen were killed.

The survivors tried to placate the victors, saying they were sorry for what had happened and would be honored if they came home to the Seven Caves, which were now the victors' caves. They asked to be allowed only to sit at the entrance. But they planned at the first opportunity to take possession of the caves again.

The half-brothers particularly hated Misty Snake. They conspired with his brother Apantecutli to kill him. One day in Sand City the Lord of Canals, aided by Xolotón, Little Quail, and Cuilitón, Little-Painted-One, murdered him. They hid his body in the sand.

The Plumed Serpent asked them where his father was. Eagle Collar, the King-Buzzard, whispered to him that they had killed his father and had buried his body in the sand.

The Plumed Serpent recovered his father's body. In anger and sorrow, he built a great temple in his honor and called it the Mountain-of-the-Misty-Snake.

This angered the survivors, both the four who were left of the quintuplets and those of the Four Hundred. Several came to the Plumed Serpent and asked why he had dedicated his temple to Misty Snake instead of to them, saying that in addition to offending the Rabbit and the Snake, he had angered the Jaguar, the Eagle and the Wolf. All were powerful gods.

The Plumed Serpent was surprised, for they really hated

all these rival animal gods, but he promised to appease them. Calling the animal gods to the temple, he told them that his aunts and uncles wanted him to dedicate his new temple to them, not to his father, but that they must help him kill his unpleasant relatives. To do that, his aunts and uncles had to believe that he and the animal gods were still enemies.

Promising they would not be hurt or killed, he persuaded them to let him tie them all together by the necks. The ones who would die would be his uncles and their friends. He would sacrifice them on the altar in honor of the animal gods.

The Plumed Serpent called upon his friends, the rats, to gnaw a secret passage through the wall so he could reach the summit of the temple unseen.

His uncles showed up with Little Quail and little Painted One, eager to rededicate the temple. They smiled when they saw the trussed-up Jaguar, the Eagle, the Wolf and other animal gods snarl at the Plumed Serpent. At once they started for the summit to make holy fire on the altar.

The Plumed Serpent untied the animal gods, then slipped off through the secret passage. He hastened, before the others could arrive, to make the holy fire with sticks in honor of his father.

Angered by this insult and trickery, his uncles rushed to the top. Lord of Canals led the charge, but he slipped and fell on his nose. The Plumed Serpent smashed his head with a stone, and the body went bumping and tumbling down the steep face of the pyramid. In the same way the Plumed Serpent got rid of the others, also Little Quail and Little Painted One.

He blew his trumpet to call the Jaguar, the Eagle and the

Wolf. He shut them up inside the upper temple and stupe-
fied them with fumes of burning chili. After tormenting
them, he opened their breasts and removed their hearts. So
he came to rule supreme in the temples and the palaces.
After a series of quick victories in many other places—The-
Place-Where-Turtles-Abound, the Place-of-Green-Waters,
the Painted Meadow, the Place-of-Slaves, the Place-of-
Broken-Skulls, the Place-of-Deer-Heads, the Place-Where-
White-Sapotes-Abound, and Hollow Place, he and the
Toltecs ruled the whole country.

*It was a religious war, a civil war, in which both the ani-
mal and the Stone People's gods were overthrown, and
Quetzalcoatl, a newcomer, imposed his own cult. The
Plumed Serpent at the head of the priestly caste and new
Toltec invaders of Anahuac—the story seems to tell us—
tricked the popular northern leaders and set them off
against the militia—the animal gods—and vice versa.*

CHAPTER 7

Flight of the Dog-headed God

The animal gods, originally worshiped at Teótihuacán, the Place of the Gods, were wholly dethroned only after repeated struggles. One such god was called Xolotl, Two-Stalked Corn, or Siamese Twin, an unreasonable dog-headed god of malformed births and monstrosities. He ran about with his crippled hands and feet doubled backwards. His eye sockets were empty, for when the animal gods were first driven off, Xolotl wept so much his eyes fell out. While the gods were discussing what to do with him, he raced off. The victorious gods pursued him.

Terrified, he hid himself among the stalks of a dense corn field. As the God of Monstrosities, he changed himself into a cornplant with a double stalk, a *xolotl*. He shivered in fright with the slightest breath of air.

His pursuers dashed into the field. Catching sight of the trembling twin plant, they knew this must be the xolotl they were after. As they started to seize hold of it, Xolotl tore himself out by the roots and ran away clumsily on his twin stalks. He hid himself among the fleshy leaves in a maguey field. There he turned himself into a *mexolotl,* or double-bodied maguey.

The gods soon spotted him. The fugitive began to weep. His tears were sweet, like the aguamiel, or honey water of the maguey.

His efforts to escape were so strenuous that he split down the middle. From the heart a winged bird darted out, a *huexolotl,* or Big Twin, a turkey-cock. It flew atop an adobe wall and fell gobbling into a corral among chickens and turkeys.

Peering over the wall, the gods were attracted by a turkey that spread out his tail with greater majesty than the others, which must surely be Xolotl. Anyway, they said they could make sure by killing all the birds.

The frightened creature flew over the adobe wall between the houses and took refuge in a kitchen, where he fell among the utensils with a loud racket.

The housewife had just been hunting for her stone *texolotl,* Stone Twin, or two-legged chile grinding stone. Now, at the very spot where the turkey mysteriously vanished, she saw the sought-for implement.

"Oye!" the gods called to her. Had she seen a turkey go by?

She said he had indeed flown in there, but had turned into a chile stone.

She tossed it over the fence. It fell on the head of a laborer tilling the garden. Previously intelligent, immediately he became stupid, turning into a *xolopitli,* a twin-swallower, *i.e.* split brain, a half-wit.

Where was the chile stone that fell in his garden? the gods asked.

The poor man laughed in a silly fashion, saying he had just eaten it!

The half-wit had the twin stone inside his body. They would have to kill him to get it out.

But from his mouth came forth a fantastic animal, neither lizard, frog nor fish, but a bit like all three. It was an *axolotl*, a Water Twin, a sort of salamander. It jumped into a garden rain tank and disappeared.

The gardener, no longer foolish, asked if they wanted the creature. He set everybody bailing out the water until the tank was almost dry. In the mud squirmed water snakes, eels and salamanders. One salamander fought so desperately to get out of the pool that he was easily caught. The poor animal god now had nothing in which to transform himself; he had exhausted all his powers of enchantment. He had transformed himself into *xolotl, mexolotl, huexolotl, texolotl*, and *axolotl*; Double Cornstalk, Maguey Twin, Turkey Twin, Stone Twin and Water Twin; and had converted a peasant into a Twin-Eater, a half-wit. Now he was lost.

One of the gods cut him in two with a sharp obsidian knife and tossed the pale blood toward the four cardinal points. The body was then thrown contemptuously into the mud.

Xolotl was the last of the animal gods to be dethroned in Teótihuacán. Thereafter the Sun and Moon and the Plumed Serpent had no rivals on the high temples or the heavens.

Centuries later a Chichamecan emperor called himself Xolotl—so the heavenly and earthly legends have become confused. King Xolotl led the main Chichemec invasion into Anahuac, the Valley of Mexico, finally set up his capital in Tenayuca, near the present Mexico City, where he built one of the finest snake pyramids in Mexico—a double pyramid corresponding to his name, in honor of Tlaloc, the River God, and Tezcatlipoca, the Black-Mirror-that-Smokes.

❖　❖　❖　❖　❖　❖　❖　❖　❖　❖

CHAPTER 8

Wise Man
of the Toltecs

When the Plumed Serpent first appeared from the sea, he was "white, tall and strong, broad of forehead, hair long and black, and he had a thick round beard."

The Toltec king, whose capital was in Tula, received the stranger cordially. The Plumed Serpent proved to be wise in the arts and sciences. He systematized the religious calendar or holy "daybook," the 260-day *tonalpalli*. He instructed the Toltecs in the art of working silver and cutting precious stones. The realm prospered. It was an age of abundance. The calabashes were thick as one's arms; so huge were the ears of corn that only one could be carried on a man's back. The vegetable plants grew to the size of trees. The cotton sprouted in every color so it no longer had to be dyed.[4] Many new birds, with rich plumage, sang sweet melodious songs. Peace smiled upon the land. It was Tula's golden age.

And so the Plumed Serpent gained full ascendancy and accumulated great riches; houses of silver and emeralds and

[4] See page 199.

turquoise and shells and fine feathers. He surrounded his new houses and temples with new wondrous trees, called cacaos. He taught the people to use the beans for making *chocolatl*, a frothy brown beverage, which they flavored with cinnamon. He built a magnificent pyramid with 51 square columns.

His most magnificent round residence was the House of Feathers. Like all his round dwellings, it symbolized the whirlwind and the four quarters from which the winds blow. The east apartment, facing the rising sun, was decorated with inlaid gold and bright yellow feathers. The west apartment, looking out upon the setting of the sun, was sheathed with the glistening plumage of the Blue Bird, woven into tapestry hung upon walls inset with jade and green jewels. The south apartment was decorated with snow-white plumage, translucent seashells, mother-of-pearl, encrusted in solid silver bricks, dazzling in the sunlight. The north chamber, of red *tezontli* lava stone, was hung with brilliant red tapestries.

The Plumed Serpent became a personage of mystery, he showed himself rarely in public, preferring tranquil seclusion. Lackeys and pages guarded all entrances to prevent any interruption of his studies and holy duties. He prayed constantly, fasted often and did penance. He was a model of purity and honor.

So venerated did he become that even the enemies of the kingdom made pilgrimages to swear fealty. He gave orders to the king and was obeyed as though he were the real ruler.

From time to time, he delivered prophecies to his people.

"The day will come when white bearded men from the east will seize these lands and substitute new gods."

Though many faithful disciples adopted his doctrines, he made many enemies. The regular priests hated him. The gods themselves became incensed at the way he set himself up as one and supreme. They decided to ruin him by making him sin publicly and thus become a general laughing stock.

They told Tezcatlipoca, Smoky Mirror—a bold and attractive newcomer among the gods, who headed the new Chichemec invaders of Anahuac—to dedicate himself to mortifying and befuddling the foreign priest, the Plumed Serpent.

The powerful dark god lowered himself to earth on a spider's thread as an aged man named He-to-Whom-We-Are-Enslaved. He asked for an audience with the Plumed Serpent, saying he was a stranger from abroad who wanted to speak with him. He said he had a picture of him that he wished to show him.

After the customary four messages, he was taken into the presence of the Wise One. The Plumed Serpent asked where he was from, and Smoky Mirror said he was from Nonoaco, near Lake Texcoco on the royal highway.

Quetzalcoatl invited him to be seated and asked to see his picture.

The disguised god held his Moon Mirror up before the Plumed Serpent. "Look at yourself, sir."

The White God contemplated himself. His face was full of wrinkles and sores. Horrified, he pushed the mirror aside. How was it possible that the Toltecs looked at him with tranquility? His appearance was frightful! He said that no one would ever see him again, he would remain shut up in his palace forever.

The Black God was disconcerted, for this would spoil his scheme to disgrace the Plumed Serpent publicly in Tula.

He said he could soon fix the White God so his faithful subjects could see him. He had cosmeticians paint the god's face various colors and adorn him with quétzal plumes. Transformed, he looked like a beautiful youth.

Looking into the mirror, the Plumed Serpent smiled with satisfaction. Eager to show himself in public, he journeyed into Tula.

Changing his disguise and accompanied by other gods, the Black God saluted him graciously and led him to a prepared banquet of vegetables, tomatoes, chiles, beans, ears of corn and pulque from the finest magueys. The Plumed Serpent ate with great relish.

His hosts urged him to try the pulque. He declined, saying that he was sick and that it might injure him.

After much urging, the Plumed Serpent tasted it carefully with his finger, found it fresh and fine-flavored, and asked to be served a small amount.

He drank and drank again, five times in all. He felt full of vigor and joy and imagined himself really young again. He became completely intoxicated.

Smiling secretively, they asked him to sing them a song.

The Plumed Serpent sang:

> They say I'm going to leave
> My house of rich plumes,
> My house of coral,
> Ai, ai, ai!

In the midst of all this pleasure, he recalled a beautiful woman, Mat-of-Quétzal-Plumes, and ordered that she be sent for. She came at once, and drank pulque until she, too, was tipsy.

The next day the Plumed Serpent recalled the previous night and his heart tightened with shame. He had been drunk, he had sinned. Nothing could wipe out this stain from his name and his high office. His anguish was so complete that no one dared try to console him. He wept bitterly and every day he grew more melancholy.

He decided to leave Tula and the Toltecs. He could live there no longer.

❀ ❀ ❀ ❀ ❀ ❀ ❀ ❀ ❀ ❀

CHAPTER 9

The Flight of the Plumed Serpent

Quetzalcoatl ordered a black coffin and lay down in it. He wished to die. But after four days he emerged from the coffin and arranged for his departure. He buried his wealth, burned his houses, changed the cacao trees into mesquites, liberated his birds. They flew before him singing. Before him also went all his musicians, singing and playing to alleviate his sorrow.

The second night out he flung himself on the ground and leaned against a large tree. Telling his pages to bring him a mirror, he gazed into it and sighed. Yes, he was old, old, old . . . For this reason the place came to be called The Old-Place-of-Trees.

He sat down to rest, this time on a stone. On getting up he left there the imprint of his buttocks and hands. The place was thereafter called Temacpalco, Hand-Prints-on-Stone. Looking back toward Tula he began to weep. His tears fell upon a rock and melted holes in it as though it were butter. It became The-Place-of-The-Perforated-Rock. He shot an arrow at a *pochotl*, a mahogany tree. It went through the trunk and turned into a second *pochotl*, forming a gigantic cross, symbol of the four winds and the four sun movements. One day he played ball, and where he traced off the court the lines became deep ravines.

At Coaxoán, Place-of-Snakes-in-Water, the disguised gods overtook him and tried to get him to return. They wished to humiliate him still more, but mostly they wished to discover his many secrets and where he had hidden his treasure.

They could not prevail upon him to turn back. He intended to travel to Tlapallán, Place-of-Sacred-Waters, then on to the Heaven of the Sun, saying that his father, the Sun, had called him and was still calling him.

They asked that he leave behind his arts of refining and forging silver and of working stones and wood, and painting and making plumed cloaks.

The Plumed Snake refused, so they despoiled him of what wealth he carried with him—his precious stones and his wrought metals. The White God threw what he could into a fountain, which thereafter was called Cozcapa, Water-of-Precious-Stones.

In another spot the enemy gods succeeded in making him drunk again. He awoke, hoarse and miserable, and tore out his hair, and that place was called Bald Head.

Passing across the snow divide between lofty Popocatépetl and Ixtaccíhuatl, his companions and disciples died of cold. He went on, lonely and weeping.

At last he reached the sea. There he contemplated his image in the water and saw that it was beautiful once more.

But as he gazed across the waters, whence he had come in an earlier time, he sighed deeply and resolved to die. Why keep on living if his rule had ended? He lit a great pyre on which to throw himself. Clothing himself in his most festive and richest robes, adorning himself with gold and precious stones, as the flames leapt high he flung himself into their midst.

Birds assembled to watch the sacrifice of that mysterious and good being, the White Lord who had fled from Tula pursued by the Black God, birds of every hue red, blue, gold and yellow, emerald-green. The singing birds came, too, and sang during that tremendous moment. Finally, when only the flames remained, the ashes of his heart stirred strangely and out of the flames rose something splendid—a star!

It rose up and up majestically, like a diamond globe, but owing to the brightness of the sun it was invisible for several days. Then it was seen shortly before dawn—the Morning Star. It was called Tlalhuitzcalpán-Tecutli, Lord-Who-Shines-in-the-Fields-and-on-the-Houses, Lord of Dawn.

Some say the Plumed Serpent built his pyre on the lofty summit of Citlatépetl, Mountain of the Star (Mount Orizaba). Others say he journeyed to Yucatán and there taught the Mayas the calendar and how to construct their fine edifices. Still others declare that when he reached the sea he vanished over the horizon on a raft of snakes.

How and when, if ever, he reached the golden realm of Tlapallán, the Heaven of the Sun, no man can tell. All that man really knew was that he promised to return in the year Acatl, five centuries later—the year the Spaniards came.

The legends of the Feathered Snake reflect the religious and political wars of the Toltecs. The stories tell of the rise of the Toltec empire, the Toltec supremacy over less ad-

vanced peoples, over their totemism and their animal gods. The imperial cycle was completed when the Plumed Serpent was in turn driven out by Smoky Mirror, the favorite god of the Chichimeca; the invading Stone Men, more primitive folk moving in on a realm grown decadent with rulers who had forgotten the welfare of their people.

The flight of the Plumed Serpent is the dispersal of the Toltecs. His journey to Cholula on the road to the coast is very likely the story of a great Toltec migration when the people penetrated far into Guatemala and Nicaragua.

The Plumed Snake was also an astronomical symbol. The whole legend is an imaginative personification of the phases of the Morning Star.

The foreign white god appeared from the east by way of the sea; thus appears the planet Venus. He lived in a silver palace of emeralds, shells and coral and comes forth in the gold of dawn and disappears in the fire of twilight.

At times the god shut himself up to do penance. Periodically, while the star is changing from the Morning Star to Evening Star, it ceases to shine, i.e. it shuts itself up in its palace of penitence.

Tezcatlipoca, the Moon, the Smoky Mirror, was in constant conflict with Quetzalcoatl, the Morning Star, pursuing him in the heavens. The Moon, who is also Night, in the end overcomes the Evening Star, by offering him a dark drink supposed to confer immortality, but which merely increases her sorrow and nostalgia—that period of gloaming when the wind and light die away, and clouds spread their dark mantle over the mountains. The Moon is a mirror, engraved with the figure of a rabbit, i.e. the sagging features of drunkenness, spots and lines, sores and wrinkles. Frightened at gazing upon it, the Evening Star decides to disappear. Once more, the two heavenly bodies confront each other. The White God adorns himself with plumes and colors to celebrate his amorous union with the sea and the earth.

The fair woman, Green Mat, represents the Earth of criss-cross corn and maguey fields. The Mexicans always pictured them as a woven mat. Beautiful Plumed Serpent and Mat-of-Precious-Feathers are locked in each other's arms; this is the rhapsodic, twilight setting of the Evening Star.

In the Great Aztec Calendar Stone, the plaited symbol of the earth is shown united thus with the Plumed Serpent, just as were the two lovers of Tula.

The shamed god hid out for four days—the time necessary to convert himself into the Morning Star—temporary death in the coffin and resurrection.

He arrived at the sea where it touches the sky, and his image was beautiful once more, for he had become the Morning Star, rising from the sea.

But the Sun approached. The dawn and its clouds were converted into a red conflagration, and the Plumed Serpent flung himself into oblivion of their leaping brightness. The dawn birds gathered around, singing to salute the new day. With the coming of the Sun, the Plumed Serpent ceased temporarily to be the Star of the new day. The cinders of his heart stirred only after the seven days necessary for him to appear once more as the Evening Star. The prophecy of the White God was nothing more than the prophecy of his own reappearance in the East. A majestic symphony, all of it, one of mankind's most beautiful epics.

With the coming of the Spaniards that prophecy became

realistic in a different sense. The disaster, then, really was cosmic. The gods really died then, overcome by the monotheistic Christian God of War with words of peace in his mouth.

❋ ❋ ❋ ❋ ❋ ❋ ❋ ❋ ❋

CHAPTER 10

The Black Mirror that Smokes

With the arrival of the Chichimeca in an ever-growing tide, the Dark-Mirror-that-Smokes, that is Tezcatlipoca, came to play an increasingly important role. As the Moon, Tezcatlipoca was represented as a smoking circle.

His image was carved out of obsidian, or volcanic glass, of a dark green color. He had white spots on his forehead, nose and mouth; his face was banded yellow and black. Two pendants hung on either side of his cheek, one silver, the other gold; and in the lower lip was an emerald disk with a blue feather. His hair was held by a plaque of gold, terminating in a gold ear, toward which extended small gold tongues, for he listened to petitions and prayers.

From his neck hung a shell-ring ornament, and on his wrists were bracelets of gold. Tied to his ankles were twenty bells of gold. On the left ankle, a deer's foot symbolized swiftness and agility, for he was also the God of the Hunt. His richly adorned sandals were gold and red; and his red and white cape was bordered with varicolored roses. He held four arrows, as a sign that he knew how to punish wrongdoers. In his left hand he held a fan, a round sheet of brightly burnished silver—the Moon—and green, red and yellow feathers—reflected rays. In the mirror he saw what happened on earth, all the deeds of all mankind.

Occasionally this mirror was attached to his head; or it replaced one of his feet, for he had lost one foot owing to the premature closing of the doors of the nether world. At the other times one foot was shown as a stone knife. He was then known as Iztli, the Knife-God, the god of human sacrifices. When he appeared with bandaged eyes he was called Ixilacoliuqui, Lord-of-White-Ice-and-Snow. He was sometimes red, and in this guise was known as Camaxtl, God-of-the-Hunt. In this role he was greatly venerated by the semi-independent people of Tlaxcala. Tremendous hunts were organized every year in his honor.

The Black God never grew old. He was always young and strong. He had great power over worldly affairs; he gave or denied individual riches; he was the god of providence, or chance, beloved by gamblers.

He taught mankind how to make fire. Placing the pointed end of a hard cylindrical piece of wood in a hole in a flat soft piece, he twirled it between the palm of his hands, creating a fine dust which smoked and smouldered and, when breathed upon hard and long, produced flame. People seized the burning wood, felt its warmth and ran to place it on their hearths and on their altars to burn incense to the gods.

The perforated wood was called *tletzxoni*, That-Which-Throws-Fire; and the cylindrical stick, *tlecahuitl*, Stick-of-Fire, and the entire apparatus, *mamalhuaztli*, Fire-Borer. This was also the name of fire. The Black God, after marking out the Milky Way, descended to earth and became the actual Fire God.

One of Smoky Mirror's names was Yoalli Ehecatl, Night Wind—a usurpation of one of the Plumed Serpent's attributes. He wandered the streets at night in search of evildoers and for adventure and love. Seats were placed at the crossroads for Night Wind's comfort. Sometimes Smoky Mirror took the form of a coyote, which ran before a traveler to warn of danger ahead—robbers or some accident.

One of the Black God's most frequent forms was that of a skunk. If a skunk took refuge in a house it was a sure sign of sickness, death or misfortune. If anyone was squirted on by this animal and spat in disgust, his hair would turn gray. If he were squirted in the eyes, he would become blind.

Sometimes the phantasm was a dwarfed woman, with hair reaching to her waist, who walked like a duck. If one tried to lay hold of her she vanished, only to reappear close at hand.

At other times the phantasm was a death's head jumping over the ground with a great hollow noise. If one fled from this skull, it bumped along behind in pursuit; if one tried to get hold of it, the skull jumped from place to place, eluding capture.

When loud blows were heard at night, as of someone cutting wood, the Aztecs said they were made by the *Yoaltepochtli*, the Night-Axe, another name for the Black God. Anyone who followed up the sound came upon a bundled-up figure that ran from place to place until the curious one grew exhausted. To his horror, the pursuer would discover the queer figure had no head and an open breast, the palpitating heart visible. When the flaps of the wound opened and closed, they sounded like a chopping axe.

The phantasm would call him by name and ask what he wanted, promising him whatever he might ask for.

The pursuer might then beg the phantasm that he be rewarded with riches or be given bravery to shine in battle. Often the phantasm gave his interlocutor a magic maguey thorn, telling him to depart. But if the person followed the phantasm and demanded more thorns and received them, he would take as many captives in battle as he was given thorns, and would be honored as a rich, brave and worthy man.

If the pursuer succeeded in tearing out the heart of the phantasm and wrapped it up in a handkerchief, in the morning he would find some valuable object. However, if charcoal or dirt were found, the bold one was doomed to bad luck and misery. The person too cowardly to follow the sound of the axe would lose all he possessed, including wife and children, and suffer every conceivable misfortune.

For a long time, in order to win followers, the Black Mirror had posed as an animal god. When the animal gods were driven out, he pretended to kill himself, leaving his cape to a follower who wandered about blindly. On a sandy beach of the sea, the god appeared to him three times. Telling him to approach, the god ordered him to go to the House of the Sun and bring back singers and musical instruments to make a festival.

But how could he possibly go to the Heaven of the Sun, the devotee asked.

Just then the Sun lifted its golden disk above the eastern horizon. The God ordered him to go there at once, while he was leaving his house.

But how would he ever cross the sea, he asked the Smoking Mirror. How could he dare demand anything from the Sun?

The god taught him a sweet song, had him do penance, and go to the edge of the sea. There the Black God cried out to the great swordfishes, to the powerful turtles of the sea, and to enchanting mermaids to make a bridge over which his emissary might pass to the House of the Sun. "Swordfish! Turtles! Mermaids! Come forth from your crystal houses!"

Innumerable swordfish lashed the sea with their gigantic tails. Millions of black turtles burst above the surface and stared at the devotee with their little parrot-billed heads. From the spray came forth legions of mermaids, singing sweet melodies.

The swordfishes told the devotee he could use their backs to get to the House of the Sun. The sea turtles told him that their shells would carry him to the House of the Sun. The mermaids told him they would carry him there in their arms.

And so a bridge stretched over the waters farther than the eye could reach. The devotee walked over it without stopping. The land was lost to sight, the mountains disappeared, he saw only sky and water. Standing at last beneath the balconies of the House of the Sun, he sang the sweet song taught him by Smoky Mirror.

The Sun listened with ecstasy, as did all the other inhabitants of the East. Coming to his senses, the Sun became alarmed and ordered the people to cover their ears, not to let themselves be seduced by such a mortal.

But many were in such ecstasy that they answered with

songs of their own. Playing their musical instruments and singing, they descended to the bridge formed by the sword-fish, turtles and mermaids and followed the courier till they all reached dry land.

They brought with them the *huehuetl*, a big leather drum, and the *teponaztl*, or wooden tambor. Quite rightly early peoples considered these and other instruments of divine origin.

Once on land, the devotees made a great festival with the divine singers, musicians and dancers from the House of the Sun. Always thereafter the festivals of the Black Mirror were celebrated with song, music and dance.

❁ ❁ ❁ ❁ ❁ ❁ ❁ ❁ ❁

CHAPTER 11

The Courtship in Tula

After the Dark-Mirror-that-Smokes had discredited the Plumed Serpent, he sought to discredit Huemac, Big-Hand, the ruler of Tula, who believed in the Plumed Serpent.

The Black God took the disguise of a rough mountaineer and squatted down naked in the market to sell green chiles. He said his name was Tohueyo.

The lovely daughter of King Huemac, gazing out from the palace windows overlooking the market, was struck with admiration for the stranger. She had long been courted by the young nobles of the realm, but had rejected them all. The king had rejoiced. He loved his daughter so much that he could not bear for her to leave his side.

Now the princess was really in love, but with a rude foreigner from the mountains. She shut herself up in her quarters to weep. She grew dreadfully ill.

Her maid told the worried king that it was lovesickness for Tohueyo, the seller of green chiles.

The king ordered angrily that Tohueyo, who went about selling green chiles, was to be brought to him immediately.

But Tohueyo was not to be found anywhere. The king sent his servants to the mountains to look for him. They failed to find him, but he reappeared in the market quietly seated beside his green chiles. At once he was brought into the presence of the king, who asked where he came from.

He had come from the mountains to sell green chiles. The king asked why he did not put on a decent loincloth, and cover himself, with a cape. Tohueyo shrugged. It was not the custom in his country.

The king said that his daughter had fallen in love with him and was sick. How should he punish him?

"Slay me if you wish," replied Tohueyo.

"My daughter would die. Bring back her health and happiness by marrying her."

The mountaineer said he was only a poor devil who had come down from his lair to sell green chiles. He preferred to die.

The king refused to listen. Tohueyo was forcibly bathed, his hair was cut, his body dyed like that of a noble. He was made to wear an ornate *maxtli*. His shoulders were covered with a rich *tilmatli* adorned with precious feathers, the finest regalia obtainable. He was married to the princess at once. And so the humble vendor of green chiles, the rude mountaineer, came to be the son-in-law of the powerful ruler of Tula, the mightiest monarch of earth.

The people were outraged. Black indignation marked the faces of the nobles. The ladies of the court snubbed the princess and her consort.

The afflicted ruler called in his principal warriors. "I know what everybody is saying," he said, and explained that he had married his daughter to Tohueyo to save her life. He was no fonder than anybody else of this stranger of base birth, he declared. After talking to his councillors, he ordered that Tohueyo be taken off to war to the land of the Coatépecs, where he was to be abandoned so he would be killed.

The warriors obeyed with pleasure. They left for war against the Coatépecs, the Snake Hill people. With them marched King Huemac's new son-in-law.

They made him stay with servants, dwarfs, women camp followers and lame folk, told him to remain there while they went to fight the enemy on Snake Hill. Shamming inferiority, the Toltecs retreated in a wild rout toward the place where they had left Tohueyo. Tohueyo's defenseless companions trembled with fright.

He told them to fear nothing, that not a single Coatepecan would be left alive.

The treacherous Toltec warriors fled back to Tula and reported to King Huemac how they had left Tohueyo all alone to do battle, accompanied only by pages, dwarfs and the lame.

The king was pleased. No longer would he be shamed by having such a son-in-law, a rude vendor of green chiles.

But the report was premature. At the battlefront Tohueyo again reassured the pages, dwarfs and lame folk. When they were surrounded, he assumed the most terrible aspect of his god-head, uttered loud war cries and hurled himself upon the Coatépec army. His war club, inset with sharp obsidian knives, flashed in the sunlight with a thousand strokes of death. The entire army fled, leaving the field strewn with bodies.

The news soon reached Huemac, who grew frightened

when he heard that Tohueyo, the victor, was marching back toward the capital with his pages, dwarfs and lame folk. He ordered that his son-in-law be received with all the pomp prescribed by law for returning heroes. The king headed the reception in person.

The nobles were humiliated. They were obliged to carry their most splendid shields and emblems and to receive the conqueror, the despised Tohueyo, with loud shouts of simulated joy.

They painted his body red and yellow—an honor reserved for those distinguished in battle. They tinted the bodies of the pages yellow and painted their faces red, adorned them in princely fashion, and escorted Tohueyo and his followers into the city with dancing, flute-playing and singing. In the palace they placed gorgeous plumes on his head.

Huemac told him to rest and enjoy himself. Everything he wished he had only to ask for.

Tohueyo asked that a great dance be held for all the people of Tula in Texcalapa, River-of-Cliffs, and sent a courier to invite his mountaineers of Tzatzitépec.

Vast numbers of Tulans attended—so did the mountain folk, the Chichimeca. It was impossible to count them all.

The dance began. Tohueyo sang a song which only the mountaineers could understand. He was giving them secret orders in the Chichimeca language.

The revel went on till midnight. By then everybody was gay and intoxicated and, as couples danced along the edge of the cliff, they were shoved over by the mountaineers upon the jagged rocks of the river below. The crowd was so great that few noticed that the dancers were plunging to their

death. The Black God turned all who fell into stones; he turned them into Chichimecas, or Stone People.

The survivors tried to escape across the bridge. This the Black God destroyed, so everybody fell into the swirling water. These, too, were changed into rocks; they were changed into Chichimecas, the same race as the mountaineers from Tzatzitépec. And so the Stone Men were the new conquerors, the new rulers.

As if in celebration, the neighboring volcanos burst into eruption. Great flames and smoke whirled frighteningly into the sky. Grisly apparitions swarmed over Tula, making terrible gestures. The frightened, sorrowing Toltecs hastened to make sacrifices upon their high altars. They made them now to the Black Mirror.

CHAPTER 12

The Plagues of Tula

After the departure of the Plumed Serpent, Tula's prosperity steadily declined. Evil signs warned of approaching disasters. Bad weather and droughts gripped the land. King Huemac decided to risk all in a ball game with the Tlaloque, the little rain gods. He put up as a stake all his fine stones and his precious feathers. They, too, put up fine stones and precious feathers.

Huemac won. Greatly chagrined, the Tlaloque treacherously substituted for their precious stones and feathers a tender ear of corn on the stalk.

Incensed, Huemac upbraided them, refusing to accept the paltry payment. Where, he demanded, were their fine stones? Their fine plumes? "As for this worthless object—take it away with you!"

"Very well," they said. They smiled malevolently and handed over their fine stones and precious feathers. Big Hand, they swore to each other, would pay dearly.

Bitter frost spread over Toltec land. Hail fell knee-deep; crops were battered down. Even during the major festival of the gods the hail kept on relentlessly. Soon thereafter Tula was stricken by terrible heat and drought. The plants withered—all the trees, the nopals, the magueys, everything. Dust swirled, rocks came down in landslides. Every growing thing throughout the land was destroyed.

Terrific cloudbursts followed; streets were flooded, houses washed away, people drowned. The tempest swept through the countryside, wrenching out trees and buildings. Loathsome toads invaded the valley and the homes, devouring everything. Locusts descended in clouds.

The Toltecs began dying of hunger. Their prayers to the gods went unheeded. Huemac used up all his precious stones and feathers, including those won from the Tlaloque, to buy food. Finally, all the slaves were sold to get bread and fowl. At last, the Toltecs began selling people into slavery. At the fountains of Taloc, by the Hill of Grasshoppers, Chapultepec, they first sold an old woman, then others, just to get a little food.

In the water of the spring, a Tulan saw a tender ear of corn, ripe for eating, exactly like the one Huemac had scornfully refused to receive four years before. The Toltecs ate it ravenously.

From beneath the water a small Tlaloque emerged, then vanished in the water, but soon reappeared with his arms overflowing with ears of ripe corn.

"Give it to Huemac," the Toltec was told. "Tell him the Tlaloque wish the king's people to sacrifice to them the infant daughter of the Aztec Lord Tezcuecuex. If this is carried out, your people will eat for a while longer."

Huemac distributed the corn to the people. He passed through Chalxiuxolhuacan. The-Place-Where-Obsidian-Is-

Quarried, handing out the tender ears, the gift of the gods, to the hungry. Through Panititlán, the Place-of-the-Canal, he went, distributing the tender ears of corn.

But Huemac saw little hope. What the Tlaloque demanded meant war with the terrible Aztecs—newcomers to Anahuac feared by all. Such was the penalty for his having refused to accept the Tlaloque's ear of corn and insisting on gems and feathers. The afflicted monarch wept grievously. Tula was lost, all Toltecs would perish.

He sent two messengers, Chicomecóatl (Seven Snakes) and Cuetlaxcóatl (Wolf-Snake) to beg the Aztec King to sacrifice his infant royal child, lest they too be destroyed. Her name was Quétxalxóchitl, Precious-Flower-Feather. Her father was greatly saddened.

The Tlaloque appeared and told him not to be afflicted, to deliver her to the Toltecs without fear. He was to uncover his tobacco gourd and smoke with them in peace. The gods would gladden the heart of his child. Only the Toltecs of Tula would be destroyed.

The Aztecs fasted four days, then the king took Precious-Flower-Feather to Pantitlán, the Canal of Sacrifice. Her heart was given to the Tlaloque.

In the land of the Aztecs, where drought had also struck, it now rained four days, night and day, and edible plants, corn and beans and squash sprang up.

The Toltecs received rain also. The plants multiplied magically by twenties, by forties. There was plenty to eat. This was in Two-Reed Year.

But the Plumed Serpent was no longer there to advise them, and things again went from bad to worse. Drought struck again in the first Flint Year of the twentieth century of the Fifth Sun. The Toltecs almost ceased to be a nation. Huemac, broken-hearted, hopeless, entered Tzincalco, House-of-the-Tender-Corn-Ear, never to return, and the Toltecs of Tula were dispersed far and wide. Some went as far off as Central America.

Remnants of the Toltecs finally took up their residence in Tula again and briefly flourished under the rule of King Tecpancaltzín, Lord-of-the-Clan-House, son of Tohueyo. But their day in the Sun was almost over.

CHAPTER 13

Discovery of Pulque

After Lord Clan House had ascended the Toltec throne, a noble relative of the royal family discovered the drink pulque, made from the sweet juice of the maguey. Proudly he called himself Papantzín Lord Pulque. He took his lovely daughter Xóchitl, (Flower), to offer the king a jar of the divine beverage.

The king was vastly pleased with the drink and the bearer, too, and begged him to bring more.

Flower came back, this time with her old nurse. Her chaperone remained in the waiting room while Flower went in alone to the monarch. He ordered his courtiers to retire. He quaffed the foaming white brew, then ardently made love to her.

The nurse was sent off with a note to inform Lord Pulque that the monarch wished to place Flower in the care of matrons to be educated. The king rewarded him with great riches, palaces and whole towns.

Flower was taken to a royal country seat near Tula where she was dressed in fine raiment and jewels and waited upon by numerous servitors. She was closely guarded and could not communicate with the outside world, not even her parents. She and the king were married, but, for reasons of state, secretly. Not even her parents and kinfolk were told.

Lord Pulque lived in anxiety for three long years. Public rumor finally told him his daughter had a child. Disguising himself as a villager selling things of little value, he presented himself at the country seat. Giving a servitor small gifts, he was permitted to pass inside to see the walled-in gardens.

He came upon Flower, carrying her child in her arms. He greeted her joyously. "By chance, does the king keep you here to take care of children?"

It was her child, she admitted, but she did not disclose her marriage. With tears and pleadings, she finally won her father's forgiveness.

Lord Pulque went to the court and boldly and angrily upbraided the king. King Clan House placated Flower's father with still more generous gifts and swore that her child would ascend the throne.

In due time the marriage was announced, and the king gave a great feast. Her father was made a high officer of the court. Thus did Son-of-the-Maguey become the Crown Prince. When forty years of age, Clan House decided to abdicate in his young son's favor.

The latter changed his name to King Topiltzín—Lord-Constable-of-the-Year-One-Reed.

After Son-of-the-Maguey grew up, he seemed different from other Toltecs. His features were odd. His long kinky hair, wound about his head, gave him an extraordinary appearance. People were reminded of the prophecy of an ancient priest, the author of the Divine Book, the Teoamoxtli:

"The Toltec monarchy will come to an end when a king with kinky hair, worn in the form of a tiara, ascends the throne. Nature will produce monstrous aberrations, rabbits with deer horns, hummingbirds with rooster crests."

These prophecies had seemed incredible. It was believed that the empire would last forever. But here in the royal family had appeared Son-of-the-Maguey, with kinky coiled hair.

But he ruled with such energy and justice that the dire prophecies were all but forgotten. All too soon, however, Lord Constable became proud and cruel and turned to vice. His rule became a shameful, unendurable tyranny. The laws were relaxed or perverted; morality and the old virtues vanished. The country disintegrated.

One of his attendants killed an unusual animal. "What a strange rabbit!" exclaimed the king.

"It has horns!" added a courtier.

"Deer horns!" cried a third.

The news flashed through the city, causing alarm. Presently a royal senator caught a hummingbird with a large crest. It was examined by the soothsayers.

"A hummingbird with a rooster's crest!" exclaimed the eldest. "This was foretold by our greatest priest. Prepare, all of you, to suffer catastrophe!"

The king appealed to the gods with prayer and sacrifices. He ordered universal penitence. But calamities soon struck.

Floods and hurricanes destroyed the fields. A terrible heat wave brought drought that shriveled the crops. Next came frosts and intense cold; later, hailstorms and blizzards destroyed fields and woods. Hardly had agriculture revived than clouds of locusts ate every green spear; other insects ate the planted seeds. A congress of Toltec wise men assembled at Teótihuacán, the Sacred City. Taking the form of a giant, Smoky Mirror rushed into their midst, seized them in his huge hands and dashed out their brains against the ground.

Next, workers found an abandoned infant crying on a mountainside, white, blond and beautiful. The king and his courtiers were upset. "This child does not belong to our race," exclaimed the Lord Constable. "Whence has it come? Who are its parents?"

The high priest and sorcerers were called in. A bad portent! They decreed that the child should be killed and examined.

The infant was found to have no heart, no intestines, no blood. The body gave off a pestilent odor, and those who smelled it died.

"Take the body away to the mountains where it was found," ordered the king. "I don't want ever to see it again."

But when a rope was looped about the body, the infant could not be moved an inch. The rope snapped, and those hauling at it fell down and died.

When others tried to pull it away, it moved so rapidly it passed over them and they, too, perished. A third time it was tried, and once more it could not be budged. They tied the body with eight ropes, putting two people to each rope. Old and young pulled, and in this way, they managed finally to drag it to Itzocán—Place-of-Obsidian. They snubbed the ropes over a jagged outcropping and left the body dangling in the air. Several persons, caught in the rope, also perished.

News came that enemies were preparing to invade Toltec territory with large armies. The king sent ambassadors with expensive gifts to sue for peace. One gift was a ball-game set. The stone through which players tossed the ball was intricately carved and encrusted with jewels of fabulous worth. Just to carry this magnificent gift required sixteen thousand men and a journey of forty days.

The enemies received the presents with great pleasure, but peace negotiations were fruitless. Soon Toltec territory was invaded. The people, though prostrated by calamities, hastened to enlist, young and old, even women. Valiantly the Toltecs tried to defend their country, even aged Clan House and Flower herself, took their places in the ranks. Flower organized a regiment of Amazons. They died bravely in the front lines, but after a terrible three-year battle the Toltecs were crushed.

Son-of-the-Maguey fled and hid in a cave. Soon he betook himself to paradise, to Tlapallán, the Sun Heaven, and never returned.

The remnants of the Toltecs of Tula fled into the marshes of Texcoco and the fastness of the mountains. The Empire was at an end. Thus was the vengeance of the Smoky Mirror fulfilled. The Chichimeca, the Stone Men, took over the whole realm.

CHAPTER 14

Left-legged Hummingbird

Huitzilopochtli, Bright Burning Bird, the Left-legged Hummingbird, God of the Aztecs, had been the guiding deity for them during long centuries of migrations, often through hostile territory. The trials, the warfare, made the Aztecs turn ever more to him for protection.

The fearful Hummingbird was one of the four creation gods, sons of Tonacatecutli, Lord of Sustenance. He was the most valiant and the cruelest of the four.

After the four gods had finished creating the minor gods, the world and mankind, the Hummingbird, a mere skeleton then, remained hidden in the silence of the sky. He took little part in the creation and did little during the periods of Toltec and Chichimec ascendancy.

But the Aztecs called on him frequently and they became his chosen people. At a crucial moment in their wanderings, he presented himself on earth as a warrior.

For this purpose he chose for his mother the goddess named Coatlicue, Serpent Skirt. No one was better suited to be the mother of the God of War. Her aspect was terrifying.

There were writhing serpents about her face and legs, and she wore about her neck a collar of human hands and hearts.

She already had four hundred children, the Centón Huitnahua, the Southlanders. Only one was a girl, Coyalzauqui, Golden Bell.

Snake Skirt was sweeping the temple on Snake Hill. A bunch of brilliant colored feathers fell at her feet. She picked them up, exclaiming delightedly, "What beautiful feathers!"

She pushed the feathers through her belt into her skirt remarking, "Perhaps the feathers were sent to me by the gods," and continued with her task.

When she had finished sweeping the feathers had disappeared. Puzzled, she went home. There oddly enough, she again felt the feathers, sinking their sharp quills into her flesh.

One day she told her sons: "I must inform you that you are to have a new little brother, whom you must love a great deal."

They cried spitefully: "We don't want any brother!" Golden Bell cried, "We would rather see you dead!"

She was beautiful, this ill-tempered daughter, with gold adornments in ear and nose; on her head she wore a beautiful scarf adorned with bright flowers and snailshells.

She and her jealous brothers abandoned their mother, going off sullenly into the mountains. Golden Bell brooded bitterly. Angrily she shook the golden bells, "Our mother does not love us. Let us kill her."

Only Cuautlicac, Eagle One, indignantly rejected the criminal project and hurried to warn his mother. "My brothers intend to kill you."

She wept and wept. Once more she felt for the bunch of feathers beneath her belt.

"Don't hurt me, mother mine," came a voice, "and don't be frightened, Little Mother, I shall defend you."

Putting on their war insignia and binding up their hair in battle style, the sons seized their weapons and bundles of darts and, led by Golden Bell, went to their former home.

Only Eagle One, the good son, was by Snake Skirt's side to defend her, one against four hundred.

The voice within her skirt was heard again. "Little Mother mine, from which direction are the four hundred coming?"

"They are coming from Tzompantitlán, the Place-of-Skulls, and have reached Coacalco, the House of Snakes."

"Where are they now?"

"They are in the place called Apetlac, the Reedy Swamp."

"And now?"

"They are on the plain."

"And now?"

"Half way across the plain. I can make out their arms."

"And now?"

"They have crossed the river."

"Where are they now?"

"They are coming up the hill."

"And now?"

"They are here!" cried Eagle One.

Serpent Skirt felt the bunch of feathers fall. They changed into a handsome tall warrior, full-grown, clad in noble armor. But curiously his left leg was very thin and covered with hummingbird feathers.

His face, with its blue forehead, appeared between the distended beaks of a helmet of green feathers, in the form of a hummingbird's head. A terrifying blue snake coiled over his nose and cheeks, the tail embracing his neck. His body was stripped with bars of blue, and he wore blue sandals. His cotton padded coat of mail was green-plumed and gold-adorned. In his left hand he carried a shield with a red border and yellow feathers. In the center a quincux of white cotton tufts represented pineapples, darts, arrows, and a battle mace surmounted by a gold pennant.

The Ramírez Codex, as told in the *Treatise of Rites and Ceremonies*, describes the War God seated on a blue bench —the heavens—with carved wooden serpent heads at the four corners. He had a blue forehead, "and over the nose was a blue band from ear to ear. On the head was a rich plumage . . . made like the beak of a small bird [the hummingbird] of highly burnished gold, and the green turkey feathers were copious and very beautiful . . . In the left hand was a shield with five pineapples of white feathers forming a cross; around it, yellow feathers like tassels, and above it a gold pennant, heaven-sent insignia . . . of memorable victories . . . in his right hand he carried a staff a blue and undulating serpent."

The four hundred were upon them, he stamped his foot, and a warrior sprang forth from the earth. He stamped a second time, and the huge blue fire snake, Xiucoatl, symbol of lightning, wisdom and magic—the "death-ray," writhed into being.

Said Huitzilopochtli to the warrior: "Hurl this fire snake and destroy the bad daughter, Golden Bell."

Golden Bell burst into flames as though struck by lightning.

The Hummingbird then attacked the four hundred, killing many and putting the rest to flight. Four times he pursued them relentlessly around the mountain.

"Mercy! Mercy!" cried the fugitives.

But the Hummingbird struck them down from behind, one after another without mercy, until he had flung the last of them into the deepest ravines of the mountain.

From then on he carried his "death-ray," his fire-snake, which made him invincible.

The Hummingbird went to the houses of the defeated ones, seizing their wealth and putting it all at the feet of his mother.

The tale records the struggle between Aztec factions. The military party sought to put the Hummingbird, or War God, above all others.

"Mother mine, I have punished your evil sons, and I bring you their treasures. Bless me, now, because I am going to make war on all the enemies of the kingdom." He went to war and became a hero, and forever after sat on a throne of blue snakes.

❀ ❀ ❀ ❀ ❀ ❀ ❀ ❀ ❀

CHAPTER 15

The White Land

Cuauhcóatl, Eagle Snake, the royal historian of Emperor
Moctezuma Ilhuicama, described the early home from which
his people had migrated to Anahuac. "Our fathers inhabited
a joyous realm known as Aztlán, Place-of-Whiteness. From
the middle of a lake rises a hill called Culhuacán, so named
because it has an overhanging summit. In this hill were a
number of caves where our forefathers lived . . . for a
great while . . . They enjoyed any quantity of ducks of
every species, of herons, of water crows, and water-hens
and widgeons . . . They enjoyed the song and melody
of birds with red and yellow heads. There they enjoyed
many kinds of handsome large fish . . . They enjoyed
the freshness of the trees along the shores and the fountains,
surrounded by willows and meadows and large beautiful
rose-trees. They traveled in canoes and made floating
islands on the water where they sowed their corn, chile,
tomatoes, sweet-grass seed, beans and every kind of plant
which we now use and which they brought from there
. . . Seven were the caves in that hill, so that the place was

often called Xicomoztoc, Seven Caves. One Aztec legend has it that mankind was created in the Place-of-Seven-Caves.

In each cave lived a tribe or gens, seven Aztec tribes, speaking the same language. One tribe worshiped Huitzilopochtli, the Left-Legged Hummingbird.

But though Aztlán was bountiful, the Aztecs were frequently attacked by jealous tribes who carried off some as slaves. These attacks increased in number and after one bloody conflict a bird, unknown to those parts, alighted on a tree and repeated his cry continuously—*tihuique, tihuique*—which in Aztec means, "Now let us go; now let us go." Huitzitón, Burning Bright, who was then captain, told the people that the bird was calling them to some great happiness.

The Hummingbird spoke through the priests, the Tlamacazque: "My people! Leave this place where you now live! Take your arms, your jewels and utensils and travel south and in the spot I shall designate, build a great city. It shall be your capital and the mother of a thousand cities. There you will be strong, rich and happy."

Obeying, the people crossed to the mainland, carrying their god in a tabernacle. He gave them firm instructions: "These are the things you must do: First, you must go adorned with jaguar skins and eagle plumes; you must go with the impetus of the jaguar and the valor of the eagle. Take with you, too, the holy flame-water, the arrow, the shield. These things I shall give you, and you shall find need for them; they shall bring you food, everything you need. You shall go terrorizing; you shall go defeating your enemies; you shall go conquering; you shall go destroying all peoples you encounter in the chosen land. On your way make sacrifices to me and to Tlaloc and to all my friends, to the gods you already know."

Four armed brigades were formed: the Tiacuán, the Valorous Ones; the Oquichtín, the Males; the Tequihua-que, the Warriors; the Cuatziqueque, the Strong-Armed Ones. Each had special dress, insignia and arms. The migration was headed by the priests of the sacred fire, followed by regular priests who guarded the tabernacle and distributed all rations. The leader was called Yaotequía, He-Who-Must-Fight-Against-Enemies. He was aided by four captains, *axcacautín*. By his side marched their chief priest, Stone-Mirror-Snake, Tezacóatl.

Fighter-of-Enemies made them spend two years preparing implements of war, shields, clubs inset with glass blades, long sling-darts, bows, glass-tipped arrows, leather and cane armguards.

When they set out on the march, the Hummingbird told them: "I wish to lead you to a place where there are beautiful lakes, with crystalline translucent waters, in which is serenely reflected the blue of heaven, where swim myriad fishes with brilliant gold fins, where there are herons more beautiful and whiter even than those of Aztlán's splendid lake, on whose banks grow limber reeds you may weave into mats on which to sleep tranquilly and rest from your long journey. Search among the islands and the reeds until, on a mound sticking up from the water, you see a nopal cactus, and on this an eagle devouring a serpent. There halt; for that is the place I have chosen for you to lay the foundations of your great imperial city."

Their departure was in the year 1064, and they reached

the valley of Mexico four generations later, in 1168. It is
claimed they crossed the Colorado River and remained
awhile in a warm valley. Next they encamped on the banks
of the Gila, finally penetrated down the west coast of
Mexico as far as Colima, then through the sierras to Mich-
oacán.

Eight other tribes were also emigrating. These inquired,
according to an Aztec account, written down by the
Spaniards, "Gentlemen and honored sirs, where are you
bound? We are disposed to accompany you," said the
tribes, "let us go on together."

They made a solemn treaty, and all the tribes took to the
road in formal procession, according to the directions of
Hummingbird. By nightfall they arrived at the foot of an
enormous tree against which the Aztecs placed the tabernacle of their god.

They were eating ravenously when a great noise issued
from the tree. Thousands of woodmen seemed to be hack-
ing furiously at the interior of the trunk. Terrorized, the
Aztecs scampered for safety as the tree split apart and the
big branches fell in two opposite directions. Miraculously,
the Hummingbird's tabernacle was uninjured.

"Be calm," he told them. "This is a sign that I am not
pleased at the company of the other tribes. You are my
chosen people and only you do I wish to guide to the place
where you are to found your city, which is to be the heart
of the world." After a brief pause, he added sternly: "Tell
the eight tribes they must go his separate way—just as the
tree has fallen." And so each went by a different route.

The Hummingbird told his people: "Henceforth you
will march alone always. You will be called Mexicans." He

ordered them to wear distinctive insignia, bolls of feathers, attached with turpentine paste or pine resin to their cheeks and ears.

They were resting, after having traveled far, when two parcels fell into their midst. In one they found a precious translucent stone. He who held it in his hand claimed it. "It is mine!" Another cried: "I picked up the package!" Still another: "I saw it first!"

The group divided into angry bands, when a priest appeared and asked, "What is the matter, Aztecs?"

He was informed of the unusual occurrence. "I marvel at your lack of brains. Two parcels fell? Perhaps the other holds something far more valuable."

Inside they found only two sticks. "*Quía!* Bah!" They threw the sticks to the ground and went back to quarreling. "The stone! The jewel!" they shouted, clenching their fists.

"Be calm, O Aztecs! Give me the objects and I shall distribute them justly." To one group he gave the jewel, to the other the two sticks.

Those receiving the stone were filled with delight. Those who received the sticks bowed their heads in disappointment. "What are these good for?"

"Look, stupid Aztecs," said the priest. Seating himself on the ground, the sticks between his open legs, he placed the hard pointed stick in the hollow of the softer wood, gave it rapid twirls. The hole turned black and wore away into a fine powder which began to smoke. He twirled the stick still more rapidly. Sweat ran down his face. Finally the softer wood burst into flame.

The Aztecs clapped their hands like children. Those

who had received the precious stone were now put out, "Wise father, give us the enchanted sticks. What good is the stone?"

The priest shook his head. "From this day you all are possessors of fire. Learn from this, O Aztecs, to prefer the useful to the pleasurable."

But the quarrel could not be healed. Those who received the jewel went their own way. Those who had received the sticks remained the true chosen people who founded the Aztec Empire.

❀ ❀ ❀ ❀ ❀ ❀ ❀ ❀ ❀

CHAPTER 16

The Vanished Lake

After many adventures, quarrels and divisions the main body of the Aztecs reached Tula where they were received hospitably and were allowed to settle nearby. The chiefs selected the Coatépec, Hill-of-Snakes. Their first care was to erect an altar to their deity. He told them: "I wish to give you, O Aztecs, some idea of the future site which I have destined for your city. Turn aside the nearby river so a lake will surround this hill."

Everyone set to work. The shores soon became covered with grass and flowers; grain and reeds lifted up their stalks toward heaven; soft-petaled white lilies, others yellow as gold, shone like starry constellations. Innumerable fish with bright fins flew about like metallic fireworks. Blue, yellow, red and white insects quivered in the grass. Swarms of sweet songbirds with beautiful plumage hung their nests in the trees. White herons came.

Snake Hill, with its bright gardens, seem to float on the blue mirror of the waters. In the clear depths were reflected the beautiful colors of that smiling settlement. It was another Aztlán. The people rejoiced that their migration and wars were over and they talked of making this serene place the permanent home of the race.

Years later the priests, at the orders of the Hummingbird, finally ordered renewal of their journey. Few people really wished to leave. Here they had built their homes and lived happily in plenty. Children had been born here and had grown up. Still the word of the Hummingbird was law. It was a serious matter to ignore his wishes. Golden Bell, who it seemed was alive after all, headed the faction wishing to remain. Nobody would budge the priestess, and more and more people were beginning to listen to her.

Inflamed with anger, the god cried: "Warn all those who object to my commands that tomorrow I shall take vengeance on them!"

At midnight a fearful noise shook the air, as if a legion of human skeletons were dancing frantically; the earth rocked, the hill quaked like a willow leaf and the lake sighed bitterly. When the people's terror was greatest, a voice, vibrating like a sword, terrible as a lightning bolt, resounded in the vast cavern of night.

"I am Huitzilopochtli, he who gives you victory over your enemies; he who has destined you to build a city that shall be the head of the entire world. My command is: Power and wealth for my obedient sons; terrible punishment for the disobedient . . . unto the last generation. Rise up, my people! . . . Cross over the rocks and through the woods . . .This is not the place I promised you. Where is the cactus and the eagle? . . . Listen

closely! The new sun will shine upon the caravan of those
who follow me. Punishment shall strike the wrongdoers."

When dawn silvered the clouds and extinguished the
stars, the faithful Aztecs looked back upon a scene of utter
desolation. The dikes of the lake had been broken into a
thousand bits; only a small creek of muddy water flowed
through sluggishly; plants lay covered with mud; millions
of dead fish turned up their brilliant scales; thousands of
birds flew about screaming.

Above, on the rocks of the hill, sprawled the bloody
bodies of the leaders of the rebellion. Golden Bell was
naked, her hair matted with gore, her face bruised and pur-
ple. Her heart had been torn out.

Father Sun rose from behind his shield of hills and hurled
down his powerful arrows, like a great fan of gold. And so
day came, rich in color, smooth as the softest plumage, and
when the priests ordered the march resumed, not a single
survivor demurred.

The Aztecs reached the valley of Mexico at Tzompantitlán, Place-of-Skulls, northeast of the lakes. The Aztec Princess was married off to the son of the chieftain there, who
joined the Aztec tribe. In due time their son Huitzílhuitl
—Burning Bright—became their leader.

They lived four years near there till hit by a terrible epi-
demic of *cocoliztli* (perhaps smallpox,) then went from
place to place suffering attacks, sickness, famine and other
troubles. For four years they settled in Xaltocán, Place-of-
Sands. They worked their way around the lakes, living
from four to eight years in various localities. In Cuautitlán
—Place-of-the-Eagle—it is claimed, they invented pulque.

They were allowed to pass through ancient Atzcapotzalco, Place-of-Ants, today a Mexico City suburb, then lived for periods in five other places, the last being Tacubaya, (now another suburb) then took over Chapultepec, Grasshopper Hill, which they fortified.

In the meantime, the priestess Herb Flower, driven out during the migration through Michoacán, had borne a son called Copil, Child-of-the-Sceptre. The injustice done to her filled the youth's heart with lust for vengeance.

Hearing that the Aztecs were in Chapultépec, Copil went about among surrounding peoples making bitter propaganda against the intruders—pernicious folk, wicked, despotic, with evil and perverse customs. So fiery was his hate campaign that all the peoples joined in a solid front to do away with those bloody evildoers. He spied on them from Tepotzinco, High-Hill-Place, a little hill in Lake Texcoco.

The Hummingbird, who saw everything, called the Aztec priests together: "Copil, son of Herb Flower . . . is preparing to harm my people . . . Go to High Hill without waste of time, kill him and bring me his heart."

The head priest selected a group of warriors, who captured Copil without a fight. Stretching him out on a naked rock, they tore out his heart and took it to the Hummingbird.

Said the god: "Go to the lagoon as far as that cane brush you see there and throw the heart into the center of it."

Where the heart was cast, there sprang up a spring and a cactus plant. Where Copil was sacrificed, where his blood ran down over the rocks, there burst forth another spring of boiling water, which still flows.

The neighboring peoples attacked the Aztecs at once and drove them from the hill. The fugitives lost their chieftain and many of their women.

A few fled into the Texcocan swamps, but most had to go into serfdom under the powerful ruler of Culhuacán, Place-of-the-Twisted-Hill. King Cox Cox, The Pheasant, made them live on land that abounded with snakes. He did not think they would survive, but the Aztecs cooked and ate the snakes with gusto. "What pigs they are!" exclaimed the king. "We shall have nothing more to do with them." The Culhuas mocked at the shrine of the Hummingbird and flung excrement into the temple.

After several years, not liking their presence so close under his nose, Cox Cox settled them in Tizapán—Chalk Place, near present San Angel—a barren lava spot of cactus, scrub mesquites, where little could be grown.

After years the Aztecs escaped. Harassed and persecuted, they ran hither and yon. They returned to Grasshopper Hill, but were driven out and re-enslaved by Cox Cox. But when he was at war with the Xochimilcans, Folk-of-the-Floating-Gardens, he armed the Aztecs to help him. The Aztecs rushed in valiantly, turned the tide and executed the prisoners on the spot.

As a reward, the Aztecs asked the king to give his daughter to be the wife of the chieftain. When Cox Cox came to attend the wedding, he found the Aztecs had sacrificed her to the gods and had draped her skin on a priest to impersonate the goddess Toci.

Lord Pheasant determined to exterminate every one of the Aztecs. They had to flee, and for another half century or so were pushed from pillar to post, living in a dozen places. Finally they were driven en masse into the swamps of Lake Texcoco.

❉ ❉ ❉ ❉ ❉ ❉ ❉ ❉ ❉

CHAPTER 17

The Founding
of Mexico City

The Aztecs had halted in many places. Old people had died, grandchildren were born, grew old and died. Great-grandchildren grew up, grew old and died. Great-great-grandchildren grew up, grew old and died. And the Hummingbird had kept saying, "Go on, go on."

Now they wandered among the desolate swamps. Some settled on a little island in Lake Texcoco, Place-of-Sands. The rest, under their chief priest, Tenocha, Thorn-Cactus-on-a-Stone, entered deeper among the reeds, using poles to vault across the worst places, until they came to a large hummock that was deserted except for frogs and snakes, ducks and eagles, birds and butterflies. It was a little island called Tlatlcocomulco, where a spring of beautiful clear water bubbled forth between two white rocks surrounded by white willows. The Aztecs were marveling at this when white frogs emerged one after another. The meadows about seemed white, and the sheen on the emerald lake about was dazzlingly white.

The Hummingbird appeared, saying: "Now you will be

satisfied. Remember: I sent you to kill Copil, evil son of the sorceress, and to throw his heart among the canebrakes of this lake. His heart fell upon a stone, from which sprang forth a cactus, a cactus so large and beautiful that an eagle lives on it. There he stretches, a serpent in his mouth, his wide powerful wings receiving the warmth of the sun and the freshness of the mornings. All about him you will find green, blue, red, yellow and white feathers of the beautiful birds this eagle has captured. That Place-Where-you-Find-the-Eagle-on-the-Cactus you will call Tenochtitlán, Place-of-the-Cactus-on-a-Stone."

Everybody prostrated himself to give thanks. Dividing into groups, they entered the dense growth of the lake, and true enough, an eagle on a cactus, its wings spread toward the sun, held a splendid snake with gleaming scales. All about was a carpet of bright feathers.

They made reverence to the eagle. "Why," they cried, "do we merit such a blessing as this? Thanks be to our lord and creator, Huitzilopochtli! We have found the home for our city." They danced with delight, and the priests performed many ceremonies.

The Aztecs told still another story. Two high priests, Axolohua and Cuauhcóatl, went among cypresses, junipers and reeds to seek the great eagle. Vaulting over the pools on long poles, on dry ground they came upon the cactus and the eagle. All around the spot, green water sparkled like emeralds.

Axolohua suddenly sank out of sight in the water. His companion waited in vain for him to reappear.

Twenty-four hours later Axolohua presented himself safe and sound. Seized by an occult force, he had been

carried to the bottom of the lake. There he had met
Tlaloc, the Rain God, who said: "Welcome to my dear
Huitzilopochtli and to his people. Say to all the Aztecs
that this is the place where you are to establish the seat of
your power, where your descendants shall be glorified."

The jubilant people hurried to prepare the foundations
of the future Queen City of Anáhuac. First they constructed a humble chapel for the god, then drove in poles
on which to build cane huts with reed roofs. The small
settlement was divided into four clans. *This was in 1324 or
1325.*

*In due time a larger sanctuary was built. Finally the
great stone pyramids rose within the enormous snake-wall
compound where the magic fountain still flowed.*

*So was founded Tenochtitlán—Mexico—the Place-of-
Cactus-on-Stone, the Belly Button-of-the-Maguey, the
birth-scar of a mighty valley— the city which was to gain
mastery not only of the lake but the whole of Anáhuac
and of Mexico even as the god had promised.*

❀ ❀ ❀ ❀ ❀ ❀ ❀ ❀ ❀

CHAPTER 18

Where Water
Is Life or Death

*On the Mexican plateau rain is scarce, often insufficient for
crops. In olden days the amount of water was the narrow
edge between survival and famine, life and death, health
and sickness, peace and war. And so the divinities of rain
and of water played a leading part in Aztec religion.*

Although Tlaloc, the God of Rain, was not numbered
among the first gods created by the Lord of Sustenance,
he came to be more important than nearly all other gods.
He was resident god at the Fountain in the Lake, a co-
founder of Tenochtitlán. His temple stood side by side
with that of Huitzilopochtli on the top of the main Mexico
City pyramid. He resided also in the fountains of Grasshopper Hill, earlier home of the Aztecs, from where later
on they built an aqueduct to bring water to their imperial
city.

The Rain God was known as Tlalocatecutli, Lord-of-
the-Wine-of-Earth, though his name was always shortened
to Tlaloc. *Tlali* means "earth" and *octli* means "wine."

His wife was Chalchiutlicue, Emerald Skirt, Goddess of

Seas, lakes, rivers and springs. From their union was born
an enormous progeny of Tlaloque (Clouds), midgets who
looked after the numerous phases of rainmaking. Each carried a pitcher and cane.

The Rain God usually lived in the highest mountains,
where clouds formed. His body was painted with holy
black rubber and he wore a mask with enormous blue
eyes, about which snakes sometimes twined. It had a huge
red mouth and enormous white teeth. The eyes represented
clouds; the teeth, rain and lightning—symbols also used in
the hieroglyphics. About his neck hung a green collar of
precious stones, and his sandals were blue. His blue tunic
was covered with a net, knotted with red flowers, and
bordered with black and red. His bare arms were adorned
with green bracelets, and elaborate gold bands clasped the
calves of his legs.

In his left hand he carried a blue shield profusely adorned
with red, blue, green and yellow feathers; and in the right,
a flame of red and gold, sharp and wavy, to represent a
lightning flash. His luxurious black hair, which fell far
down his back, was bound with reeds, though often he
wore an elaborate diadem of white and green plumes. He
rested in a semi-recumbent position, by pressing his el-
bows backwards, his knees drawn half up to symbolize the
mountains whence rains come.

Besides his altar in the great square, he had a special
temple on top of Mount Tlalocán, Place-of-Rains, east of
the lake, that was visible for miles. There his stone image
reclined on a platform surrounded by a great multitude of
smaller idols representing adjacent hills and ravines. *The
Tlaloc festival there in the Month of Drought was always*

attended by the three kings of the early triple Aztec alliance.

The temple of these Gods of Water was modeled after the upper Rain Heaven. Four salons gave on to a wide patio and four wells, each containing a different kind of water. The first held good rain, which produced fertile crops. The second contained rain that caused cobwebs and mildew. In the third were stored ice and sleet. The fourth held the worst rain, which let nothing mature or dry. Thus Tlaloc could germinate good crops or smite the earth with trouble, sending fort his legion of midget functionaries, the Tlaloque, to produce rain, lightning, cyclones, and "water-snakes" or cloudbursts. The Tlaloque filled their pitchers with whatever water was designated, which was poured out in the form of rain or hail over mountain and plain, bringing either well-being or calamity. They beat the pitchers with their canes to cause thunder.

If they broke their pitchers with their canes, the thunder was fearful and loud, and lightning was produced. If a *tepelacatl*, a piece of the broken pitcher, fell upon the earth, it was the death-ray that destroyed and burned.

The Tlaloque, so small that the eyes of mankind were unable to see them, were always on the go. They herded the clouds everywhere, now accumulating them in the peaks of the high mountains, now flying rapidly over the valleys, emptying their pitchers and making them reverberate with their canes.

The name of Chalchiutilcue, Emerald Skirt, Goddess of Running Water, came from *chalchiuhuitl* (jade, emerald) and *cueitl* (skirt), the name of the mountain which guards the entrance of Tlaxcala. Emerald Skirt was especially worshiped by those who traveled or did business on the

water; the vendors of fruits, flowers and vegetables on the canals; those who sold fish.

Emerald Skirt was full-bosomed and had a golden face. Her crown was of clear blue parchment with green plumes that hung down her neck. A medallion was suspended from her collar of precious green stones. Her light-blue blouse and skirt were adorned with sea-shells, and her sandals with jeweled mosaics. In her left hand she held a small circular red-flanged shield, centered with a water-lily leaf. In her right hand, she carried a vase surmounted by a blue cross.

Sometimes she was shown kneeling barefoot in simpler costume—a headdress of white feathers held in place by the band of a red shawl with golden tassels. Over her right ear was a white flower. Hanging down over her white blouse and the red band about her hips was a chain of precious green stones ending in a gold medallion. Her skirt was green bordered with red. All about her leaped blue watersnakes.

Emerald Skirt was especially honored along with Tlaloc, first in Drought Month, then in the Month of Succotash, when the wet season was well under way, and the first flowers showed and cornfields were green. The priests went out into the fields, gathered armfuls of cornstalks with tender ears from each garden, and took them to the small crossroad shrines. The women brought tender corn cooked in milk. Afterwards all danced and sang and feasted. At night in the temples there were sacrifices, and the following day everybody went out in canoes on the Pantitlán, Place-of-the-Holy-Canal, to the sound of trumpet and conch-shell music. Precious stones and other offerings

were thrown out, and four parchment offerings, tied to an incense burner, were tossed burning after them.

During the "God-Rest" festival, celebrated every leap year, people dressed themselves in costumes representing animals and birds and, dancing around Tlaloc's temple, mimicked their calls and cries. They plunged into a lake where they caught eels and frogs in their mouths and devoured them alive.

The Tlaloque were also honored. After temple ceremonies, the priests led a procession with music down to the lake shore, to the Four Houses of Fog. They robed and performed ceremonies for four days in each house in turn. On emerging from the fourth temple, a priest would say, "This is the Place-of-Snakes, the Place-of-Mosquitoes, the Place-of-Ducks, and the Place-of-Reeds," whereupon they all dived into the water, splashing about and imitating the cries of birds, ducks, *pipitzli*, sea crows and white and royal blue herons.

The priests returned naked to the temple, playing on their pipes and horns, and put on their robes and jewels.

In the fields, all tools, the wooden picks and spades, the nets for carrying loads, the crates, the ropes with which loads were tied on the back, were cleaned and scrubbed and placed on a platform in each home, where they were honored with food and drink, especially succotash. After the ceremonies everybody went out to the rivers to bathe, then danced in the temple courtyards or in the market. Anyone who failed to join in was doomed to punishments by Apitzeotl, God of Hunger.

There were burlesques, too. Instead of dressing up like the god, many people put on masquerade costumes and performed clownish tricks. At midnight these went from house to house, dancing and singing, carrying a large jar and begging a little succotash, with the threat of breaking a hole in the house. The frolic ended at dawn.

One Tlaloque, Opochtli, patron divinity of fishermen, invented fishing nets, bird traps and oars, and the *minacachalli*, a trident for spearing fishes or birds. In his festivals he was offered food and pulque, green cornstalks, flowers, copal incense and aromatic herbs. The celebrants struck hollow sticks, imitating the Tlaloque's pitches and canes, and carried his image over a path strewn with popcorn to symbolize hail.

Opochtli's body was stained black. About his dark face hung quail feathers. On his parchment crown, shaped into artificial roses, green plumage was held in place by a yellow knotted tassel, and longer tassels hung to his shoulders. His stole was of criss-crossed green and from his waist green papers hung to his knees. He wore white sandals adorned with four leaves and thorns in the form of a cross. His sceptre was a flower chalice, with a sheaf of arrows sticking out of it.

Napantecutli, Four Quartz, Four Times a Lord, another Tlaloque, was the god of the cane-weavers, the makers of mats, petates (reed mats), baskets and cane furniture, such as round-bottom leather-back, cane-woven chairs. This god supplied the necessary rains for the proper germination and growth of reeds and cane. He was stained black, except for white flecks on his face. Tassels, each with three green feathers, hung down his back from his black-and-white parchment crown. Over his right shoulder and crossed under the left armpit ran a white band embroidered with black flowers. His short black and white skirts were laced with seashells. He wore white sandals. His shield was shaped like a water lily and he carried a scepter of twined paper flowers.

His temple was always well adorned and swept clean by the devout caneweavers. Reeds and cane were always planted in the holy precincts, and his temple was always well provided with new mats and chairs.

The Four Quartz festival was joyous, with much eating, drinking, dancing and singing. The person giving the festival spent every cent he possessed and pledged all his belongings to make the event an elaborate affair. He would say to the god: "I shall give my all and leave myself absolutely nothing. Replenish me or leave me with whatever you wish—or nothing." A priest attired like a god, wearing a white cape, led a procession through the canebrakes. Carrying a large green vase, filled with water, he used a leafy branch to sprinkle all the celebrants.

Mountains, in the image of the chief god-mountain, being the source of water, were sacred. Tlaloc was often called Tepeyolotl, Heart-of-the-Mountain.

Popocatépetl and Ixtaccíhuatl, the two great white volcanoes, were prominent gods—husband and wife. On the summits, where man might speak face to face with the gods, the Aztecs erected temples. Images of these mountain deities were put in their plaza temples. That of Ixtaccíhuatl, the White Woman, in the main temple of Mexico, was of wood—a young girl with bright red cheeks, dressed in blue, with a crown of white parchment, painted with black designs, held in place by a silver medallion from which flowed white and black feathers. Her hair, in bangs across her forehead, hung full and free over her shoulders.

All children took part in the gay festivals of the mountains. In the temples and in every house the father would say: "Come, children, let us go wash the straw wheels." The children led the way, playing on clay flutes, to the nearest river or pond. *These wheels, small mats, well-woven and tied, used for cushions or wall-decorations, are still found in homes and churches in outlying districts, although their earlier meaning has been forgotten.*

Upright sticks, placed in the center of each washed wheel, were tipped with gobs of *tzoalli*, honey dough or joy bread, molded into miniature mountains. The first mountain would usually resemble Popocatépetl. About it clustered other smaller mountains. Each was given two faces: a human face, stained with rubber sap, the cheeks rounded out with corn tamales; the other, a triangular serpent's face. Both were adorned with sacred papers and crowned with feathers, in special honor of persons who had been drowned or wounded by lightning.

For two days, the celebrants served them food in tiny toy dishes: tamales, fried livers, hearts and sweet dough. Incense was burned. For the all-night dance, everyone dressed in white. The children played on their flutes. At dawn, a guest took a wooden knife and made an opening from which he pretended to take out the heart.

The sweet pretend-mountains were then gaily broken into pieces, and the children and elder people ate the dough of joy with as much gusto as though it really were the flesh of the gods. Some dough was saved and taken up on the flat roof to let the sun harden it into cakes to be eaten later. Grains of corn of white, black, yellow and green were thrown to the four winds to make the fields fruitful. With vessels containing corn or water, the celebrants sang, "Popocatépetl, Ixtaccíhuatl—and other honored mountains— give us abundant rains! O gods of Water and Earth, give us abundant crops!"

To the mountain fiestas were invited the *pulqueros*, the pulque-makers, who were urged always to make good pulque. But until the end of the fourth day the celebrants abstained from drinking pulque, or the honeywater from which it was made, not even moistening a finger to taste it.

The Aztecs imagined that certain sicknesses, especially those connected with excessive cold—gout, paralysis, rheumatism and muscular contraction—came from the mountains and could be cured by the mountain gods. Those afflicted asked the priests to make honey-dough images of the gods: the God of Air and Winds, the Plumed Serpent; the Goddess of Water, Emerald Skirt; and the God of Rain, Earth-Wine; also images of the volcanos: Popocatépetl, Sierra Nevada, and Citlatépetl (Star Mountain). Calabash seeds served for teeth and large black beans (*ayocotli*) for eyes. Papers gummed with rubber sap were fastened about their necks, and others were hung from cords tied to poles, so they rustled in front of the images. The images were offered pulque from a smooth, round "knife-gourd," spotted whitish green.

The night of the fourth day after the images had been made, the sacerdotes held vigil, with singing and dancing. Music was made by whistling with the small finger in the mouth, and with horns and flutes. Tamales were offered to the priests and the guests. At dawn the priests cut off the heads of the images and twisted them, and the dough was taken to the Calmecac, the House of the Priests. There everybody danced and sang all day and part of the next night, even old folk, men and women. All drank pulque. Some wept, others bragged and acted pompously; others quarreled.

So the mountain gods, propitiated, assured rain for the crops and good health for all.

❁ ❁ ❁ ❁ ❁ ❁ ❁ ❁ ❁

CHAPTER 19

Earth
and Its Seeds

After having made the waters, the gods created the fish
called Cipactli, which was converted into Earth. The hiero-
glyph of this birth of continents was Tlaltecutli, God of
Earth, riding on the back of Earth-Woman-Tlalcíhuatl—
the chief Earth Goddess, the Holy Dweller. Most beloved
was Xochiquétzal, Precious Flower-Feather, the Goddess
of Flowers, of Artists and of Love, also the benefactress of
weaving and embroidery. Those who went hunting for
wild honey prayed to her for good luck. So did those who
hunted deer with lariats. The shooters of arrows, the cutters of canebrakes for fish traps, all fishermen using traps,
hooks, nooses and spears paid her special court.

She wore gold pendants and nose-ring. Her diadem was a
band of red leather, from which waved long green quétzal
feathers. Her elaborate blue dress was embroidered with
flowers and feathers in sophisticated designs, and with red
and gold bands about the flounce. She carried in her outstretched hands bunches of feather flowers, bound with
gold ribbons. Her small shrine, erected within the large

holy compound, was lavishly hung with tapestries and featherwork, well filled with jewels and gold ornaments.

Precious Flower lived in the ninth heaven, a delectable place of fountains, rivers and flowers. There grew the marvelous tree, Xochitlicán; its sweet potent flowers, if merely touched, converted one into a happy and faithful lover. She was waited upon by many female genii, dwarfs, hunchbacks and buffoons, who prevented any man from seeing her.

Originally Flower Feather had been the wife of Centéotl, God of Corn, then of Tlaloc, i.e., Flowers married to Rain. But Tezcatlipoca, the cunning deceiver, fell in love with her and stole her from Tlaloc. He shut her up in that flowery and delectable abode. Tlaloc, scorned and sad, sought consolation in the arms of beautiful Emerald-Skirt-of-the-Lakes.

Flower Feather's farewell festival, just before the arrival of cold weather, in the Month-When-the-Fruit-Falls, ran over into the next two months. Branches and flowers were twined about all the temples, houses and streets, and people decked themselves with vines and flowers. The faithful gathered in the temple, especially painters, artists, silver-workers, feather-workers and weavers. A girl dressed as Flower Feather presided.

All danced gaily, masquerading as monkeys, cats, dogs, foxes, mountain lions and coyotes. While performing the steps they carried the various work tools. They ate honey bread painted to represent dolls, flowers and birds.

Flower Feather, also Seven Flower (Chicomexochitl), were honored in the second movable fiesta by the Brotherhood of Painters and Weavers. After a forty-day fast, blood drawn from the fingers and the eyelids was offered by the men to Seven Flower, the inventor of the artist's brush; by the women, to Flower Feather, who invented weaving. Many quail were sacrificed.

Macuixóchitl, God-of-Five-Flowers, and of Fire, was worshiped chiefly in the homes of nobility. This was the major flower festival of the year. Before it was celebrated everyone fasted for four days. If any man or woman sinned, the god punished them with diseases. Many savory foods on painted wooden plates were brought as offerings.

Another earth goddess was called Chicomecóatl, Seven Serpents, because of the seven racimes (sprays of flowers) of the corn plant and the writhing corn silk. Also, seven corn plants were always set out in each hill. Seven Snakes was a beautiful young girl wearing a red crown; her dress and sandals were of the same color—she was red from head to foot. Gold earrings glistened in her ears and a necklace of golden ears of corn, strung on a blue ribbon, hung about her neck. She carried cornstalks with double ears made from gold and feathers. To insure good crops, when the first blades of corn appeared people went out at night and lit an *ocotl* torch in the center of the field, where they sacrificed a fowl and offered bread, tamales and sweet copal. As Goddess of Cookery, Seven Snakes had been the first to make bread, tortillas and other toothsome dishes, and on her feast day the housewife carried to her altar a basket of provisions surmounted by a cooked frog, bearing on his back a cornstalk stuffed with pounded corn and boiled vegetables.

The festival in her honor and the corn god Centéotl was celebrated with feasting, dancing and music. The altars were lavishly decorated with green boughs, herbs and flowers. Girls in capes carried seed corn to the temple to be blessed—six ears each, wrapped in paper sprinkled with holy rubber sap. The arms and legs of these girls were adorned with rich plumage of many colors; their faces were stained with pine resin or tar called *chapopoctli*. They went in procession, surrounded by the crowd. No one was supposed to talk to them. If some young blood did speak, he was rebuked by one of the old women chaperoning the girls: "You speak, coward, greenhorn? Do you have to open your mouth? You had better be thinking of some exploit to rid yourself of the long hair on your neck, sign of cowardice and lack of manhood. Chicken-heart, you don't need to pipe up here. You are just as much a woman as I am. You have never left the fireside."

One of the youths would respond: "Very well said, madam . . . Never worry, I shall do something that will cause the girls to consider me a man. I care more for two cacao beans than for you and all your lineage. Put mud on your belly, scratch yourself, cross your legs and go roll in the dust. Here is a sharp stone, cut yourself in the face and the nose till blood comes; and if that doesn't satisfy you, swallow chalk and spit. I beg you to be still and leave us in peace."

When the corn had been blessed, it was brought back to the house, and the rest of the day was spent in revelry.

The male equivalent of Flower Feather was Xochipilli, Lord of Flowers, of dances, song and games. He wore a high *cocoxtli*, or pheasant crest; and in his mouth a white butterfly. His body was patterned with painted flowers. He sat on a flower throne, adorned with symbols of fertility, rain, water and the sun, and his hands and his painted face were always lifted up in rhapsodic awe. In his role as

Macuilxochitl, Five-Flower, he was the god of gambling. Aztec dice were made of five different colored beans.

Many earth divinities were worshiped by the decapitation of victims, to symbolize the reaping of the corn. In the codices these victims are represented with their heads half-severed, with two writhing snakes about the neck to represent streams of blood, rain, corn floss and other things.

Woman Snake, called Tlillán, i.e. Blackness, had a temple called Tlillán, the Black House, beside that of the Plumed Serpent in the great temple square. Only priests of her cult might enter there. The door was so small it was necessary for them to crawl in on all fours, and the passageway was so arranged that the interior remained pitch black, with not a ray of light. Her stone image had a large mouth and teeth bared ready to devour. Her hair hung free down her back. Near this temple the priests kept an eternal fire lit, and they presented themselves once a week to the emperor for food for the goddess.

If the goddess did not receive her weekly ration the priests placed a sacrificial knife in a cradle, and a woman carried it to the market place (the *tiánquiz*) where she left it in the care of a seller, to be kept until she returned.

When the woman did not return, the market woman, wondering why the child did not cry, would discover the knife. This was a sign that Woman Snake had been among them and was hungry. The market woman cried out the bad news, and the priests gathered weeping, reverently taking the knife off with them. The emperor, the nobles and all the people, thus publicly shamed, hastened to provide the goddess with her usual repast.

CHAPTER 20

Fire Gods
and Time

The Aztecs were fire worshipers. Fire was universal life. Ometecutli, Lord of Duality, God the Creator, was the fire essence, the unseen inner fire present in all beings and things, in earth and heavens. Fire was the oldest god.

Ometecutli and his son, Tonacatecutli, the God of the Fire in the Sun, were the parents of all the gods. Hence the Aztecs called Fire *tota*, from *to*, meaning "our," and *tatli*, meaning "father"—"our father."

Earthly fire was Ixcozauhqui, Yellow Face, better known as Xiutecutli, Lord of Grass, Lord of the Year, shown on the stone calendars as a bundle of grass, surrounded by the hieroglyphics of the eighteen twenty-day months, Fire and Time were closely related.

The God of Fire had his image in all temples. He wore a paper crown painted with mystic designs, and long green plumes covered his ears. Often his hair was adorned with a butterfly, whose fluttering flight was like a flame. He was naked from the waist up. On his back the Fire-Snake wore beautiful yellow plumage resembling a dragon's head.

His loincloth was gold and his sandals were tied over the instep with bright red bows. He carried a round shield with a cross of five green jadestones on a sheet of gold, and his scepter was a round plaque of gold and two golden balls, one capped with a point. To hide his dazzling face, the god looked through a slit in the scepter.

Fire God was offered the first bite of each dish, the first swallow of drink, both being tossed into the fire. The newborn babe was symbolically baptized in a fire kept burning to nourish its existence.

Since the God of Fire was also Lord of the Year, an elaborate "fire ceremony" inaugurated each new year.

Closely associated with Fire God was the Goddess of Lightning; Itzpapalotl, Glass-Blade Butterfly.

One day two deer appeared among the maguey fields, each with a double head. Two surviving Cenzón Mimizcoa (The Northerners), Xiunel (Grass-Lord) and Mimix (Lord of Fishes) took their bows and arrows and went out to hunt for them among the rocks and brambles. They built two grass huts in different parts of the field and watched all night for the two animals, and then a whole day.

By sundown they were completely exhausted, but they kept on building huts in different likely places. Still the two animals never put in an appearance. When all their food was exhausted the two hunters started to leave. Two women, who had previously taken the magical form of the two-headed deer, ran after them, calling "Señor Xiunel! . . . Señor Mimix!" asking them to drink and eat with them.

Xiunel was soon on good terms with the elder one, but

Mimix held back shyly. The younger woman, beautiful in her gold dress, called to him to come and eat with her. But Mimix went away without answering.

She made fire by rubbing two sticks together and soon had a large blaze lighting the dark forest. Suddenly Mimix came running from the dark and started to jump into the fire. The girls tried to hold him back and called to him to eat, drink and be merry, but he plunged into the flames.

The younger girl threw herself through space in her gold gown. The sky spirit Tzitzimitl, Arrow Ray, who held up the heavens, shot hot arrows at her that stopped her flight. He soon left her and she tore her hair; she tore her flesh with her nails; she wept that she had been spurned.

The Lord of the Year heard her weeping, but when he tried to seize her, she flung herself into the fire. When she reappeared, dazzlingly bright, they called her Itzpapalotl, the Lightning.

Her body was rayed with red bands; her yellow-tinted face was hidden by a dark mask. Back of her head was a yellow butterfly with a wing pattern of eyes and stars that shot out lightning rays. On her back she carried a skull decorated with five white feathers. She held a scepter and a shield, divided by a horizontal black line cutting through a red square. Her feet were eagle claws.

From her golden body burst forth the green-blue flint, the green-blue of the sky. From her golden body burst forth the white flint that makes sparks. The gods seized it and wrapped it up. Then from her golden body burst forth the yellow flint that gives sparks, the flint of sun-fire, but they could not get hold of it; they only saw it. Then from her golden body burst forth the red flint that makes sparks, the red flint of flames. They were unable to get hold of it, they only saw it. From her golden body burst forth the dark brown flint that gives off sparks, the flint of blood-fire. They could not get hold of it; they only saw it.

Itzpapalotl took the white flint, carefully wrapped it up and went toward Comalán, The Place-of-the-Comal-for-Making-Tortillas, which she easily conquered, and had the people worship the white flint as Mixcoatl, Cloud Snake, the Milky Way. Other towns were conquered and forced to worship Cloud Snake.

The Aztecs had many fire gods and fire festivals. Their celebrations, as those in honor of the Sun, tied up closely with their calendar, its cycles and its intricate numerology. The calendar was an integral part of life and religion. They studied all the mysteries of the planetary movements, carved out the secrets of the heavens, and minutely correlated their calendar with the movements of the sun, the moon, Venus and the Pleiades. The periods of time were subdivided by the Aztecs differently than with Western peoples. The Aztec hours, weeks, months and centuries do not coincide with ours. Only the years are equal. Time, represented pictorially by an arrow, was one of the great mysteries, a ruling force of the universe.

The demigods Cipactli and Oxomoco were Darkness wedded to Light; Night wedded to Day: and from this union was born Time—day, week, month, year and century, the double century, and the 260-day religious cycle. This semidivine pair, therefore, invented the famous Toltec-Aztec calendar.

Time was also symbolized as springing from Tonatiu, He-Who-Falls-Head-Down-Burning, the Sun itself, and from its four majestic movements—Nahualín. This Sun God is depicted in the center of the Great Calendar Stone, his fiery tongue extended as a sign of life, the tip in a transparent, water-filled urn containing two polliwogs and two eggs to represent fertility and life.

An arrow, Time, passes through him—the Mexican meridian, in the shaft of which were embedded, like jewels, the symbols of the weeks. He clings to the heavenly zodiac with two claws, symbolizing the inventors of time, Cipactli and Oxomoco. Each claw has nine symbols, the number of nights in the Aztec night-week, together giving the eighteen months of the Aztec year. Below the month symbols are the thirteen-day week period, also the daytime hours and the nighttime hours (ninety minutes each), the four solar thirteen-year cycles, and the fifty-two-year "century" cycle. Another cycle on the calendar stone depicts the twenty days of the month. Arrow points mark off the four-year cycles, the four winds, the four cardinal directions whence they come, and the 260-day religious cycle.

Rays glance out through seven encircling bands, carved with the symbols of time, the zodiac, stars, air, water, and lightning, and hieroglyphics of memorable dates—the whole enclosed by two linked serpents with the faces of the Evening Star and the Sun to symbolize their meeting at the completion of each 104-year double-century. This memorable stone is dated Year Thirteen Cane Stalks, or 1479, the culmination of great historical and calendar cycles in the reign of Emperor Axacayatl.

On this stone are recorded the four earlier destructions of the earth, the beginning of time, the start of the Aztec migration, the founding of Mexico City—altogether they provide a sublime summary of Aztec history, religion and philosophy, of life and time, immortality and the universe. It is a stone-carved condensation of the vast Teoamoxtli, or Sacred Calendar Book. *The great early researcher, Benaducci Lorenzo Boturini, asserts that the first major astronomical revision of the calendar was made by the Toltecs in 100 B.C.*

Each calendar year, starting on our February 12, consisted of eighteen twenty-day months, plus a five-day "idle period," the *nemontemi*. Each day of the month had a different name, so each week began on a differently named day. Thus it took thirteen months or twenty weeks, before the first day of the month and the first day of the week coincided again. This provided the religious cycle of 260 days.

Owing to the five extra days, New Year's Day could fall only on one of four days numbered according to the year: Year One Rabbit (Tochtli), Year Two Reed (Acatl), Year Three Tecpatl (Flint Knife), Year Four House (Calli), Year Five Rabbit . . . Nine Rabbit . . . to Year Thirteen Rabbit. Then the new thirteen year cycle began as Year One Reed, the next One Flint Knife, etc. Thus only after fifty-two years was Year One Rabbit repeated and in the same month. The fifty-two-year period was also significant because the religious cycle, and the day, week, and month—the solar cycle—coincided for the first time.

Every eight years was significant for the Venus cycle (584 days), *i.e.*, five Venus years, and the solar cycle (365 days) coincided. The really stupendous cycle occurred every 104 years, the double-century, for the solar count, the Venus count, the century cycle and the religious cycle all coincided. Naturally this fired everybody's imagination; it spoke of the harmony of the spheres, the orderliness of the universe, the reconciliation of mathematical irreconcilables. It suggested rhythms, form, design and purpose; it gave substance to the meaning of time; it tied the days and nights, the seasons, the crops, life itself, in with the sun, the moon, the planets, the wheel of the earth. It attested to the wisdom of the Great Spirit. It represented godhead. No people has ever solved the calendar problem with greater astronomical accuracy and mathematical and philosophical precision than did the Toltecs and Aztecs.[5]

The Aztecs believed that, after the Fifth Sun, the world was likely to come to an end again at the close of any fifty-two-year cycle—by fire, or wind, earthquake or flood: or it might be that Glass Butterfly, the Lightning Goddess, would perpetrate the destruction. Or it might come through the anger of Smoky Mirror. Hence the passing of each "century"-cycle was celebrated by an elaborate New Fire festival.

Holy fires, kept lit during the entire fifty-two years, were extinguished. All other fires were also extinguished. On the last night new fire was reproduced in the ancient manner, with the use of pieces of wood. If success attended this effort, the world would last another fifty-two years. If not, nothing would prevent the Sun and Earth from perishing. The people also destroyed their most treasured possessions. They tore their clothes and broke their fur-

[5] See page 199.

niture and utensils. Even gods and idols were hurled into the rivers and the lakes. Everything must be replaced by new objects.

Extreme anxiety ruled on the critical night. No one thought of sleeping. The sun might never rise again! And if the sun did not rise, terrible hideous figures, called Ttzitzimitli, the Sky Spirits, would descend upon earth and devour the people. Pregnant women and children put on masks of maguey fibers (*mezayacatl*), so that in the event of catastrophe, they would not turn into wild animals and devour their neighbors.

Save for the stars in heaven, the most complete obscurity reigned over the earth. A night of terror, in which all trembled, from child to grandparent—for they had no assurance that the dawn would come, that the sun would reappear.

The priests, dressed in the insignia of all the gods, marched in silent procession towards the outskirts of the city to Ixtapalapan, Place-of-Salt-Works, five miles distant from Tenochtitlán, a hill with a twisted summit, the Hill of the Star.

All the inhabitants also walked out to the sacred hill. In distant villages the people went to the nearest elevations and mountains to get a view of the Sacred Hill of the Star, to watch for the reappearance of the divine flame, the New Fire.

On the summit of the Sacred Hill, the priests waited until the Pleiades reached the exact zenith. On the open breast of a sacrificed victim, the priests then placed the *mamalhuaztli*, the sticks with which New Fire was made. The appointed priest twirled the hard stick with great energy.

The multitude below waited in fearful expectation. The most restless were those on the far-off hills. The priest, sweating and panting, worked until the softer wood powdered, smoked, took fire.

"The flame!" A cry of jubilation and relief burst from the assembled masses. The cry was caught up and carried in all directions from end to end of the vast valley of Anahuac.

From the soft burning wood of the *mamalhuaztli* was lit an immense bonfire there on the summit. As the flame leapt up in the dark night the people on the mountains in far towns danced and hugged each other, crying and laughing. People drew blood from their ears with thorns and threw it in the direction of the blessed New Fire.

Messengers quickly carried it by lit *ocotli* pine torches to the four cardinal points. On all sides, in all the villages, in the remotest provinces, in the most hidden hamlets, these carriers, chosen from the best runners and specially prepared by fasting and religious ceremonies, were waiting in relays, ready to receive the holy flame and distribute it over the empire. Racing down the hillsides, careful not to let the flames go out, these runners passed the precious fire from hand to hand until, in an incredibly short time, it was distributed to all the hamlets of the land. One by one the hearth fires and the altars were relit. Once more comforting shadows danced along the walls.

Life was renewed! Life was assured for another fifty-two years! In every house there was a festival, music and dancing and drinking, and the people ate *tzoalli*, the Bread of Joy. New hopes flowered. Everything, clothes, furniture, idols, utensils were new. Life had begun again!

CHAPTER 21

Road
of the Dead

The owl, the *tecolotl*, was the special messenger of Mict-lantecutli, the Lord of the Dead. When this bird cried over the house roof, it was believed someone was going to take sick, perhaps die. *Mexico still harbors the saying: "When the owl cries, the Indian dies." Sayings, vulgar and other-wise, and rituals try to exorcise the bird's evil augury.*

Mother Earth received the Aztec dead comfortingly on her breast. They belonged to her. Mother Earth, Cihua-cóatl, Woman Snake, often hungry, called for mortals to devour. When propitiated, she grew more kindly toward all humans, gave better crops, flaunted her flowers.

The body of the dead was placed on a *petatl*, or mat, and, if of noble lineage, a piece of precious jade was placed in the mouth; if a poor person, an ordinary stone.

The dead one was addressed: "O Son, you have endured and suffered the labors of this life, and it is proper that you be taken away, for we have no permanent life here on this earth; brief as a sun-warming is this life. We give thanks that we have been able to know and converse with each other . . . but now you are taken by Mictlantecutli and the goddess Mictlancíhuatl, to the place awaiting you. All of us will go there; that boundless region is for everyone. There will be no further memory of you. You will go forever to a dark place that has no windows and no light."

The old people and priests poured water on the dead person's head, saying, "This is the water you enjoyed while living in the world," and they placed a jar of it upon the shroud, for the dead one to travel with. Papers were cut to symbolize the various episodes of his fearful journey to Mictlán, the Land of the Dead. Each detail of that journey was minutely described by the priests as each paper was laid before the body. The red dog of the deceased was killed, and both were taken to the place of cremation to be burned by the two oldest men of the community, while mourners sang dirges. Into the flames were cast the dead man's belongings, his baskets and weapons, his trophies of battle, his clothing. If a woman, all her jewels.

The mourners gathered up the cinders, the charcoal and the bones and poured water over them, saying, "Let us bathe the dead." The ashes were buried in a round hole. Any bones remaining were placed in a jar, along with a green jade stone, and conserved in the home of the family where each day offerings were placed before it.

One Chichimec emperor introduced the custom for the nobility of keeping the corpse seated on a chair for five days, so it might be sufficiently contemplated by debtors, vassals, friends and relatives. It was dressed in royal robes, with jewels of gold and precious stones and placed upon a large chair, adorned with multicolored plumage, along with incense, perfumes, balsams and perfume censers. At the cremation, all adornments and accessories were set on fire. The ashes were deposited in a carved stone urn, inscribed with the name, ancestors, age, deeds and date of death. This urn was then placed on an elevated throne for forty days, the object of public veneration and weeping by the vassals and family, then it was sealed in a cave or subterranean vault.

Emperor Ilhuilcama Moctezuma, however, forbade cremation, and ordered his coffin to be made of solid gold and encrusted with precious stones.

The Tlaxcalans believed that the souls of nobles turned into mists, clouds, beautiful feathered birds, or precious stones; the common people into weasels, beetles, skunks and other unpleasant animals.

The passage from life into Mictlán was a fearful ordeal.

Ometecutli, after he had created the earth with its seas and forests, created the humble Road of the Dead, which led to Mictlán, the Mansion of the Dead.

Not everybody had to travel that fearsome road, for there were three special heavens, where babies, mothers dying in their first childbirth, and valiant warriors perishing in battle, were taken directly through the shades and terrors of life just beyond the grave. But all others, regardless of rank or worldly goods, whether nobles or plebeians, had to go over the Road of the Dead to Mictlán.

Both Aztecs and Greeks conceived of a river that guarded the entrance to the palaces of the nether world. The boatman of the Aztec River of the Dead was a red dog, for neither white nor black dogs could swim the big River of the Dead. Such a dog, with a red cord tied loosely about its neck, was always cremated along with the deceased.

Red-dog breeders lived in Coyoacán, Place-of-the-Breeders-of-Coyotes, and elsewhere, and there was a famous market in Acolmán.

Near Xometía, in the arid plains of Texcoco, stands today the temple of San Agustín Acolmán. The walls, toothed by semi-pyramids, rest heavily against counterbeams and supports. Around the temple huddle a number of sombre little huts, separated by narrow, cactus-bordered streets. From the towerless roof of the temple one sees the cornfields of the modern Indians.

"At the hour of Ninek," relates ancient tradition, the sun shot an arrow into this spot. It opened an earth-wound out of which emerged the first man, a strange being. He could free only his shoulder and an arm from the grip of the earth. He remained a dog and was called Aculmaitl—Shoulder-Arm—and the soil that bore him, Acolmán—Place-of-the-Shoulder-Arm.

Acolmán grew up to be one of the chief cities of Texcoco, and with the growing prosperity of the people and the increase in population in Anahuac, prosperity came to the dog-markets, for which the place was soon famous. There, from all over Mexico, people came to buy red dogs for companionship and funeral purposes.

The red dog, waiting at the River of the Dead, on recognizing his master, barked joyously and swam the master across. Otherwise the poor soul would wander restlessly through all eternity.

Beyond the river rose two toothed mountains, bumping

loudly together like angry giants, a terrifying spectacle. The dead one, confused by the noise and the strong wind, had to pick his way between the crashing giant projections. After much struggle and sweat, the terrified traveler, protected by the magic of the rubber papers in which his body had been wrapped before cremation, would get through. But his journey had only just begun.

A terrible, enormous snake lay in wait. Once his fangs and snapping jaws had been eluded, the harassed shade was confronted by a gigantic lizard as big as an alligator—a *xochitonal*—with an enormous black throat, saw-like teeth and a lashing tail.

The half-exhausted pilgrim faced another mountain, glistening as though encrusted with precious stones. Actually, the whole mountain bristled solid with sharp obsidian knees. The traveler's feet were sliced to bloody ribbons. In steep places he had to use his hands, which were sliced to the bone. He had to drag his body over these razorlike edges till every inch of him was streaming blood.

On the other side he had to cross a range of mountains enveloped in a terrible blizzard. The dead one wrapped himself up in the extra clothes buried with him, giving thanks for the foresight. Passing one crest, he found still another! Passing that, still a third! The snow obstructed the road in great drifts; sleet tore at his face; icy wind buffeted him. Eight such terrible glacial heights had to be crossed, and still Mictlán was nowhere in sight.

The dead one, exhausted, frozen to the bones, had to plod across a vast desolation swept with sleet. The violent wind tore out sharp volcanic stones, which cut into the flesh like a thousand knives—"the glass-knife wind" it was called.

Fierce Izpuzteque, Broken Face, the demon god, tore and clawed with his eagle-claws at the suffering pilgrim. Next the evil Nixtepehua scattered over him clouds of hot ashes and burning coals.

Suddenly an arrow whizzed through the air, burying itself in his body. A second arrow followed. By the time he had crossed the long stretch, his body was a pin cushion, so many were the arrows sticking into his flesh. Eight such desolate stretches—and still no Mictlán!

As he crossed the last span of the last plain, a ferocious jaguar leapt out snarling. Too exhausted to run or fight, the traveler fell terrified to the ground, screaming. The jaguar tore open his breast with his sharp claws and ate his heart.

Now he had to go on without even a heart to give him strength and hope. He fell into a pool of black water and lay there, stunned and despairing. Only after a long time was he able to crawl out.

The dead one stumbled on and on until he came to a great valley full of deep, wide rivers. On the opposite bank of the first river, was his faithful red dog again. The animal threw itself into the water and helped him to pass over. Nine icy rivers had to be crossed.

Not until then did he arrive at Mictlán, the Place of the Dead.

CHAPTER 22

Mansions
of the Dead

The pilgrim was taken immediately to Mictlantecutli, Lord
of the Dead, who sat on a throne surrounded by skulls and
bones, by perched owls and quail, and odd courtiers having
eyes the size of tiny straws. It was surrounded and guarded
by the dread sky spirits, the Tzitzimitli, they of the shining
tresses.

Mictlantecutli's face was a skull, with a stone knife instead
of a nose. His huge fleshless mouth was wide open to catch
the souls of the dead. Another stone knife was suspended
from his necklace of bones. His tunic was embroidered
with death symbols, and his shield, half red, half ash-col-
ored, was strewn with stars. He always held his hands palms
outward fingers curving upwards—the Aztec gesture meaning, "Come hither."

But the Lord of the Dead did not frighten folk, and the
Mansion of the Dead was the equivalent of the Christian
limbo. Though it was dark, sinners did not fear it. After the
frightful struggle to reach it, the place seemed like a haven,

and the dead soul was content to remain there forever in forgetfulness and everlasting peace.

It was composed of nine levels. The upper levels were dimly lit by the setting sun, Tzontemoc, The-Sun-That-Has-Set, He-Who-Has-Fallen-Head-Downward. The ninth, the deepest and darkest level, was without roads, utterly silent.

To the Lord of the Dead the newcomer presented everything which had been burned or buried with him—paper, perfumes, jewels, the red cotton thread, his cape, loincloth and clothing. Thereupon the god said gently: "All your suffering is over. Come and sleep your sleep of death."

There were three other Mansions of Death: Chichihaucuahco, Place-of-the-Tree-of-Milk; Tlalocán, Place-of-the-Wine-of-Earth; and Ilhuicatl-Tonatiul, House of the Sun.

Unweaned babies, when they died, came to a special abode, sheltered by the great branches of the Tree-of-Liquid-from-the-Breast, a beautiful region of perpetual sun, meadows, bright flowers with the loveliest perfume, and birds of every hue that sang sweet songs. Hummingbirds and butterflies sipped the honey. From the tips of the leaves of the great tree in the center of this paradise, there oozed drops of milk, which hung suspended glistening in the sun, then dropped into the open mouths of the happy infants seated in a circle below. The mother who had lost her child had her sorrow assuaged by knowing that her loved one would go to a garden of delight, the kingdom of innocence, to live a life of everlasting joy in which tears were unknown.

All persons who died "unnaturally," from accidents,

lightning, leprosy, or other ugly diseases, were destined for Tlalocán, the Place of Tlaloc and the Tlaloque, the Place of Rain, where all waters originate. This was the Moon Heaven, the place of gentle rays, illuminated by the Lord of Snails. This was a place of eternal happiness, blooming and balmy, a paradise. The dwellers in silvery moonlit Tlalocán enjoyed a second more beautiful life without suffering.

The Heaven of the Sun was traversed by the Sun each day. There went the soldiers killed in battle, prisoners who died at the hands of their enemies, victims sacrificed on the altars of the gods, and mothers who died at first childbirth, the divine Cihuapipiltín—Women-of-Children. They had snow-white faces, chalked arms and legs, golden ears. Their *huipil*, or blouses, had black wavy designs; their skirts were embroidered in various colors, their sandals were white.

The Holy Mothers, ranking equal with warriors, lived in the western part of the Sun Heaven, but despite their delectable abode, they never became reconciled to the loss of their children, and frequently visited earth to do spiteful deeds. They haunted the crossways at night, as strange cloud and air shapes, or as witches or eagles. Often their bodies were luminous. The *ignis fatuus*, fool's fire, was one of their manifestations. They injured babies and children, causing paralysis, and they could enter into living human bodies, causing sickness. On the days of the year when they descended to earth, parents never permitted their children to go out of the houses.

To avoid these evils, offerings were made in the special temple of the Cihuapipiltín and at the crossways. Food was left for them—tamales, toasted grain and bread shaped into butterflies or lightning bolts.

At the hours when the Cihuapipiltín were expected, a woman who had sinned went alone to the crossroads and stripped herself naked, sometimes cut out her tongue.

The eastern part of the Heaven of the Sun—for soldiers who had been killed and for all sacrificial victims—was beautiful with fresh green woods, delightful meadows, fields covered with fine grass, endless magic gardens with exquisite flowers that never withered.

Before daybreak the warriors of the East Heaven gave joyous shouts and shot their golden arrows ahead of the Sun—the first rays of light to shine over the earth. They continued shooting until the Sun reached the zenith.

There the Mother Goddesses waited the Sun. They, too, shot their arrows with jubilant cries. Before the feet of the Sun they laid down rich mantles woven from quetzal feathers, and accompanied him, joyously shooting arrows, until they left him in the far west.

Night began. Thereupon the Sun passed dimly through Mictlán. The Dead there awoke, arose, and running toward him, conducted him in utter silence, in order not to disturb his twilight sleep, to the gates of the East, where he awoke once more and gave light to mankind.

After four years the warriors in heaven were converted into hummingbirds—the form of the War God—and were free to suck honey from the flowers. They even descended to earth to drink the honey of the beautiful flowers cultivated by men.

❀ ❀ ❀ ❀ ❀ ❀ ❀ ❀ ❀

CHAPTER 23

Arts
and Crafts

The gods were always close to the hearthfire and work-bench. Some were the patron deities of special trades and professions. Opochtli, the Tlaloque rain godlet, looked after fishermen.

The merchants and traders, the *pochteca*, Those-Who-Flew-Along-The-Roads, had great importance. Their principal god was Yacatecutli, Lord-Who-Goes-Before-Like-a-Nose, i.e. The Guide.

Guide Nose was an ancient pilgrim with a staff. His face was spotted black and white and he wore gold pendants. His hair was tied on top of his head with whorls of quétzal plumes. His cape was blue, with a black net design and tassels of flowers and a flounce embroidered with flowers. About his ankles were strips of yellow leather decorated with seashells; his sandals were stout and richly adorned. His shield was yellow with a center of a light blue spot.

His staff was like those traders carried, elaborately carved with flowers, birds and serpents. *Apizaco was and is today famous for its carvers of canes*. The travelers also carried fans of parchment, wood or feathers, for much of their traveling was in hot regions where insects abound.

The *pochteca* also honored the Gods of Fire and of Earth, Xiutecutli and Tlaltecutli, since they often lit wayside fires for company or warmth. They revered The Sun, for good weather was helpful, and they sacrificed quail to him. Two other favorite divinities were the Goddesses of the Highway, Zacatontli and Tlacotontli, representing respectively *zacatl*, and the turpentine shrub, useful plants which grew everywhere by the wayside. The former produced the stout cord with which bundles were tied and hammocks and bags were woven; the other supplied holy sap for sticking things together and coating objects against rain. The *pochteca* made rich offerings to these various divinities.

For several days before departure, all-night banquets were held in the houses of the wealthy merchants. At dawn they buried the ashes of their sacrifices—flowers and perfumed stalks—so they would not be defiled in their absence by any unclean person, such as a thief, adulterer, gambler or drunkard.

To welcome the sunrise the merchants sang and danced with the tambor and the *teponaztli* drum. The eldest person present wished the travelers a good journey and exhorted them not to lose heart. All drank cocoa and smoked together. The merchants bathed and bound up their hair, for during trips, which might last for months, even years, they never washed any part of their bodies except the backs of their necks.

The journey began at night. Each carried his staff and fan and never looked back, for that would bring bad luck.

The caravan went double file along the outer edges of the road. Lesser merchants, who lacked slaves and had to carry their own merchandise, took the center of the road. At the end of each day all staves were tied into a bundle, representing the god Guide Nose, and were adorned with holy papers, cut to resemble the Sun. With maguey thorns, the merchants drew blood from their ears, tongues, legs or arms, to sprinkle over the sticks, then burned incense and begged the god to protect them from danger. In honor of the two plant goddesses, paper was cut into the shape of butterflies—symbols of what flies along the sides of the road.

The most used routes were marked by wayside stations, large well roofed corridors where the night could be passed comfortably.

Sometimes in distant, dangerous parts the merchants traveled with armed guards, or *tequihua*. These carried a lance in one hand and a fan in the other. At night they spied on enemy countries, slipping secretly along the streets, bridges, crossings and high points, to plan effective future attack and provide information to the emperor. *"Trade follows the flag," is no new phenomenon, nor is its converse, "the flag follows trade."*

If a pochteca died at the hands of an unfriendly folk, he was given the funeral of a warrior, a *yaoyizque*, and an image of him, carved from *ocotli* pine, was reverently burned. If he died of sickness the eyes of the corpse were painted black, the mouth circled with red, and the body was bound in white strips of cloth and put in a crate or *cacaxtli*, then hung atop a pole—to be "eaten by the air."

The successful pochteca, on returning home, often after

years of absence, brought male and female slaves—sometimes bought at the last minute at the Atzcapotzalco market, the Place-of-Ants—to give them to Guide Nose and his brother gods and sisters—named Seven Rain, Weary Flesh, Maguey Sap, Nose Leader, Leaf-Rope-Woman. These slaves were treated well, given every luxury and dressed in the habiliments of Guide Nose or his brothers and sister. After much dancing and singing they were sacrificed, in the Birth of Flowers month. But male slaves who proved to be excellent workmen and female slaves who were adept at household work or in knitting, weaving and other domestic arts, escaped being sacrificed.

Articles of commerce were male and female slaves, jewelry, earrings and necklaces, gold or silver crowns, vases, rings, lip and nose ornaments, worked and unworked jade, sea shells (natural or worked into adornments), bright colored seeds for necklaces, precious stones, coral, obsidian; bells of clay, glass, stone, gold or silver; feathers of turkeys, quail, pheasants, eagles, quetzals, flamingos and herons; also, pottery and carved gourds, carved and painted wooden plates, carved canes; tapestries, blankets, cloaks, embroidered sashes, blouses and skirts, hides or furs of deer, wildcats, jaguars, pumas, skunks, coyotes, hares, bats and birds. There were also dried meat and dried fish; maguey thorns, bone or glass needles, shark's teeth, flint or glass knives, drums, flutes, rattles, darts and lances; carved and jeweled chocolate-beaters, fibers, henequén, pita, ropes, cotton mats, hangings, blankets, shawls, *cactli* or sandals, textiles, clothing; parchment, paper and pulp; rubber, resinous pine (*ocotl*,) woods and lumber, charcoal; sapotes, chirimoyas, mangoes, pineapples, loquats, avocadoes, magueys, cherries, plums, strawberries, persimmons, papayas, guayavas, bananas, plantains, bread fruit, star and custard apples, nopales, tomatoes, olives, squashes, gourds, pumpkins, roots, tubers, cactus leaves, sweet potatoes, yams, peanuts, coca, cacao, cashew nuts, chiles, cereals, corn, popcorn, edible grass-seeds; honey, spices, cinnamon, sarsaparilla, sassafras, medicinal and odorous herbs, medicines, lemon tea, salt, tobacco; incense, copal, rubber sap, resin, chicle, ocotl, peyotl, religious charms and idols of wood, clay, glass, stone, bones, jade, gold and silver. Salt, quills of gold, pieces of jade, often served as money. Later on a few coins, stamped with images of the emperor, were used.

One of the four main groups of the Aztec migration settled in Amantlán, ward of Tenochtitlán, hence were known as Amanteca. They devoted themselves to feather work, the curing and dressing of hides, dyeing fabrics and processing furs. They erected a large temple, or teocalli, with an image of their deity, Coyotlinautl, Face-Painted-with-Gold-Bells, (or perhaps Painted Coyote), whom they had brought with them on their long trek.

Painted Coyote was always dressed in an embroidered painted skirt. His face was either stained or bore the mask of a person with long pointed gold teeth. His staff was inlaid with precious black *itzli*, or obsidian and gems. His round shield was bordered in light blue. Over one shoulder he carried a vase from which flowed forth hummingbird feathers. His anklets were of white sea shells made into bells and his sandals were woven from the leaves of the *xicotli* tree. Anyone wearing such sandals was known as an Amanteca, i.e. a feather worker or furrier.

Other gods worshipped by the Amanteca were Tizaba

(Chalk Face), Macuilocelotl (Five Jaguar), Malcuiltochtli (Five Rabbit) and the two goddesses Xiutlatl (Earth-Year-Woman) and Xilonen (Tender-Corn-Ear). Very much revered was Tepoztecatl, the patron god of the city of Tepoztlán, the Place of Copper, renowned for its feather work and metalwork. All, except the two goddesses and Chalk Face, wore coyote skins.

Twice a year fiestas were held in honor of these divinities, first of all to Painted Coyote. During the singing and dancing, people drank a beverage called *itzpachtli*, Glass-Knife-Sliced-Beer—fermented fruit juice, particularly pineapple juice called *tepache*. *This is still a common beverage in Mexico*. At the second fiesta in honor of the two goddesses, all the Amantlán women dressed up as Earth Year or Tender Corn, and the men wore feathers on their legs. Earth Year ordered that children be sent to the temple to be taught the trade.

The ward of the Amanteca was next to that of the pochteca, and the two groups usually celebrated jointly, for feather-work, leather and furs were leading articles of commerce.

The feather workers cut their feathers with obsidian knives on tables made from *ahuehuetl* or cypress slabs. They made feather capes and decorated shields for the nobility and the gods and special plumed garments for religious festivals. In the beginning they used the feathers of lake water fowl, but in the prosperous and powerful reign of Ahuizotl, when the far provinces of the south and of Guatemala and Salvador were overrun, the pochteca brought in the plumage of rich tropical birds.

The gem cutters were another important class of artisans.

They lived mostly in Xochimilco, Floating Flower Garden, the lake town Venice, where the stone cutters first emigrated and became famous. They worshiped four divinities: Seven-Thorn-She-Dog, Noble Sorceress, Five-Room House and the Corn God.

To Seven Thorn they attributed all feminine adornments, jewelry, cosmetics, etc., and upon her favor depended most of their prosperity. In her right hand she carried a scepter; in her left, a shield bearing the picture of a human foot. Her ears were of solid gold and from her nose hung a gold butterfly.

Noble Sorceress wore her hair in two disorderly parts. On her forehead was a paper-thin sheet of gold; her earrings represented stone cutters' instruments. Her shield, covered with a netlike design, and her scepter were decked out with rich feathers. Her white-and-red jacket had an embroidered flounce. She wore red sandals.

Five-Room House wore his parted hair on top of his head with rich plumes. On his temples were plates of gold and about his neck hung a large pearl. His scepter was also of plumes, but his shield was painted with red bull's-eyes. His entire body was stained red and he wore red sandals.

The Lord of Corn wore a mosaic mask. His jacket was sky-blue, and a gold-mounted jewel hung from his neck. His white sandals were tied with soft cotton. He was always seated on a throne of woven cornstalks.

To these divinities were attributed the working of precious stones, the making of earrings and lip lancets from black or white stone, glass or amber; the fabricating of necklaces, bracelets and strings of glass, metal or seed beads, the boring and polishing of jade.

Salt workers also had their patron deity. Salt played a vital part in Aztec economy, and it and chile were closely tied up with Aztec religious rites, fasts, and penance. One severe punishment was to oblige a penitent to forgo salt over long periods. The search for salt deposits went on unceasingly. It was extracted from the waters of saline lakes and from the sea. *The need for salt led to migrations, wars and trade. Salt, often exacted as tribute, was often at the root of Aztec imperialism.* Such towns as Ocoytuco, Coazxulco, Temuaque, Coajitea had to give forty loads of salt four times a year.

An important feature of the Aztec homeland was the great salt lake Texcoco, in the marshes of which Mexico City was founded. Its salt gave the Aztecs formidable trading advantages. Ixtapalapa, the Place-Where-Salt-Is-Gathered (today a modern suburb of Mexico beside the Hill of the Star, where was celebrated the New Fire ceremony), was devoted almost wholly to extracting salt, called *ixtatl,* i.e. ground white. Other large salt centers were Ixtacalco, House-Where-Salt-Is-Made, and Tequisquitlán, Place-of-Crude-Salt, or Rock Whiteness.

Salt peddlers went out over the length and breadth of the land, and then salt increased in value with each step taken up the steep mountain trails.

The salt goddess was Huixtocíhuatl, Shining Salt Woman, a sister of the Tlaloque or Cloud Gods. Following a quarrel they exiled her to the salt waters in the south. Her celestial abode was in the White Heaven of the South, the domicile also of the Plumed Serpent when he acted as Evening Star. There she invented the way of obtaining salt by evaporating water from tanks or shallow pools.

Salt Woman was white or yellow, as is some crude salt, and she wore a mitre with many green feathers. Her golden ears spread out like the flowers of the calabash. Her *huipil* and her netlike skirt were woven with blue sea waves and embroidered with colored jade. On her ankles were golden bells and white sea shells, sewn to jaguar skin, and her sandals were of colored cotton. Her shield was adorned with the broad leaves of the salt-water plant *atlacuecona*, with butterflies, and flowers made from eagle wings. Her staff, decorated with artificial flowers and quétzal feathers, threw off incense.

Since salt was not only a commodity, but often served as money, she was a favorite deity of traders. Merchants and the nobility celebrated many fiestas in her honor. On special fast days they dressed up in her vestments and ornaments.

Salt workers honored her in a hilarious garden festival. Everyone wore his finest clothes garlanded with flowers and odorous herbs, and priests came clad in full regalia. All danced to tunes and steps set by old men.

One of the most important industries was the gathering of the sweet sap of the maguey, or agave plant, which was allowed to ferment to become the frothy white beer known as pulque.

But misuse of pulque was considered evil because some persons, when drunk, threw themselves over the cliffs, or into the water to drown, or hanged themselves. Many quarreled and killed each other or abused women and children. These misdeeds were attributed to the God of Pulque, Mirror-Straw-Hair.

Mirror Hair's wife was Coatlicue, Snake Skirt, and she had many close relatives: Lord Warrior, Ice Face, Twisted

Brow, Black Water, Lord of Medicine, Lord Builder, Pulque Straw, Earth God, Two Rabbit, Lord of Copper, Lord of Gardens and others. There were four hundred pulque gods, called "Rabbits," all brothers, born of Mirror Straw Hair and Mayauel, goddess of the maguey plant. All were closely connected with moon phases and the harvest and the many ways of making different flavors of pulque and the innumerable forms of drunkenness and the vices that went along with drunkenness.

Straw Mirror was killed by Smoky Mirror, but later was resurrected. By this action, the sleep of the drunken, so similar to death, became "harmless" for men. The awakening after heavy sleep was symbolically connected with the waxing and waning of vegetation and the moon. Another story says that Smoky Mirror was lame because he had been thrown in a drunken state from heaven by his disgusted fellow-gods.

The festival of the god of the pulque makers was celebrated whenever Mazatl, Deer, the third day-sign, began the month, i.e. once every 260 days, or thirteen months. This always took place on the second day of that month, i.e. on Tochotli, or Rabbit Day. The pulqueros prepared a great leaf-decorated vat, filled with foaming pulque. The first honey water from the maguey and the first glass of each kind or pulque was offered to the god.

Little Negro Face, Ixtliltón, a brother of Five Flowers, was the deity of both medicine and pulque-drinking and he was the medical god for all children. In his sanctuary of painted boards he kept many jars and tanks, covered with slabs of wood or stone and filled with black water, *tlilatl* concoctions of brewed herbs—i.e. an apothecary shop.

When any child fell sick he was immediately rushed to the sanctuary and made to drink the black water corresponding to his ailment.

For the fiesta of this god, a priest dressed in the god's habiliments. He danced with the people to the sound of *teponaztli* and tambors, everybody chanting. The priest led them into the wine cellar, where covered jars and tanks were filled with flavored pulques, allowed to ferment for four days. All drank, then went out into the patio where covered jars and tanks contained black water. If any dirt was found in them—as straw, hair, or charcoal—the person giving the festival was a man of evil habits or a thief and was accused of being a troublemaker. The priest hid his shamed face in his cape and hurried away.

Omecatl, Two Reed, was the divinity of hospitality, since clean reed-woven mats were provided for all guests. When guests were invited in to eat, dance and sing—always in a profusion of flowers—the image of Two Reed was brought to the house by several priests. If not so honored, he appeared to the host in bad dreams, scolding him for his neglect, warning him he would pay dearly, and he would put hairs in the food and drink to annoy the guests and dishonor the host. The guests fell ill or choked, and when they got up from the banquet mat they stumbled or fell.

The god was always seated on a bundle of reeds. His face was stained black and white. A parchment crown, with a chain of jade beads, and a wide band of many colors was fastened tightly about his forehead by a tasseled knot at the back of his head. His cape had a broad flower-embroidered flounce.

In his honor, a large imitation bone was made out of

honey dough, The-Bone-of-the-God. At dawn he was punctured with glass or maguey needles, then broken into pieces, which the guests ate. As a reward during the year following this festival, the god would provide everything necessary for the enjoyment of life.

❋ ❋ ❋ ❋ ❋ ❋ ❋ ❋ ❋

CHAPTER 24

The
Talking Stone

The Aztec emperor and his peoples leaned heavily on priestly oracles, who told of the Spanish invasion and the doom of the empire even before the events.

One clear, serene night, the chapel of the Hummingbird atop the main pyramid burst into flames. Although the priests called a great multitude to extinguish it, the sanctuary was completely destroyed.

Moctezuma ordered its immediate reconstruction, and prepared to inaugurate it with imposing ceremonies worthy of the god. He ordered a larger, handsomer sacrificial stone quarried.

Stone cutters and carvers searched over the mountains and ravines until they found a stone of the desired size on a hill in the province of Chalco in a place called Aculco. They rolled it to a level spot, dressed it down and prepared to transport it to Tenochtitlán, there to be carved with the figures of the gods, sacerdotes and warriors. It was necessary to pull and push it across rough country, and great masses of people were assembled with ropes and levers. The sacerdotes, or priests, burned incense on the stone, sacrificed quail on it, and covered it with sacred papers and drops of rubber sap and copal. Dancers and religious chanters were to go ahead. Comedians and buffoons would perform stunts and tell jokes and riddles to the people. Weeks of enjoyment were in prospect.

The ropes were placed, the levers set, and the multitude hauled at the ropes and pried with levers. Nothing happened; the stone did not budge.

Again orders were given, but the ropes broke like spider threads. The levers broke like straws.

Moctezuma ordered his people to put more ardor into their task. The stone was finally brought to the edge of the lake.

By then Mexico City had grown to a vast metropolis of canal streets, boats, canoes and magnificent causeways. Drawbridges permitted the passage of boats through the canals. *So wide were these highways that the Spaniards later could ride eighteen abreast along them.*

At handsome Ixtapalapa boulevard the stone spoke: "It is useless for you to take me into the city. Listen, Mexicans, soon there will come from the East white men with beards, who will overthrow your power and seize your lands, tumble down the altars of your gods, raze your temples and substitute a more powerful god. If you take me in, I shall be despised and broken into fragments. Go to Moctezuma and tell him. Leave me, therefore, here in this spot."

The emperor angrily ordered that the stone be brought in. It was moved along the boulevard to the first carved gate.[6]

[6] See page 200.

The inhabitants rejoiced with music, dance and song, throwing incense and flowers. But on the bridge the beams cracked, hurling the stone into the lake along with many people and priests.

Divers sent to salvage the stone found no trace of it. The king was provoked beyond all reason. One man ventured to say: "If the stone did not wish to enter Mexico, it must have returned to its old hill in Aculco."

They made the long trip back to the hill. Sure enough, there they found the stone, just as though it had never been moved at all, still surrounded by the broken ropes and levers. On it were the papers and the drops of rubber and copal and the blood of the sacrificial quail. Greatly upset, the emperor sacrificed several captives to conjure away the stone's evil predictions. But the stone never reached the city.

❀ ❀ ❀ ❀ ❀ ❀ ❀ ❀ ❀

CHAPTER 25

Cloud
Arrows

The Aztec emperor when the Spaniards came was Moctezuma II, The Wrathful—the tenth in succession.

As a lad at the Calmecac, The House of Wide Corridors, he had studied the history of the Aztecs, the use of weapons, ideographic writing, astronomy, astrology, the calendar and the Tonalamatl, the sacred almanac or Book of Fate. When he was chosen to be emperor, he was humbly sweeping the steps of Huitzilpochtli's temple. He was led before the altar where he offered sacrifice by drawing blood from his ears and his legs. For his coronation his nose was pierced to receive the royal emerald.

Moctezuma spread the empire wider. He conducted campaigns, along the Gulf of Mexico and exacted tribute from 371 more cities. He reorganized the administration and punished improper ministers and judges severely.

In 1508 there appeared high in the east a luminous phenomenon, a great light, Mixpamitli, or Cloud Arrow. In 1509 the comet was seen again, a tongue of flame, pyramidal in shape, that threw off great sparks. The Indians believed it was the Plumed Serpent, the White God, whose return they had so long awaited.

Alarmed, the emperor consulted with all his astrologers and soothsayers. None could tell him what it meant, no one could allay his fears. Only wise Nezahualpilli, king of neighboring Texcoco just across the lake, renowned for his occult wisdom, could tell what it meant. But there was bad blood between them. The Texcocan had hanged one of his wives, who was Emperor Moctezuma's sister. Putting aside his rancor, the emperor invited the king to the capital, and asked him to interpret the celestial phenomenon.

The king told the emperor: "Great and powerful Lord, I do not wish to disturb your generous soul, but I must give you an absolutely truthful account of this marvelous phenomenon that the Lord of Heaven has put in the skies, burning by day and burning by night. Within a few years, all our cities will be destroyed and leveled, we and our sons killed, and our vassals overcome. Never again, if you make war on the Huexotzincas, Tlaxcaltecas or the Cholultecas, will you obtain victory. Your people will be defeated with great loss of life. Before many days you will see other heavenly warnings. But do not despair, for what has to happen is inevitable. Only one thing consoles me—my own days are short, I shall not live to see these calamities."

To test out the truth, Moctezuma challenged his guest to a ball game. Nezahualpilli confidently bet his entire kingdom against Moctezuma's three finest gamecocks, promising that if he won he would take only their spurs.

In the ball court, or *tlatchco*, Moctezuma won two games right off, and, after a harder struggle, the third also.

Overjoyed he said: "It seems to me, Lord Nezahualpilli, that I now see myself Lord of the Texcocans."

Nezahualpilli replied: "True enough, my Lord, but even so, the whole Aztec realm will end with you. Others will deprive you and me and all of us of our territories. To prove that, let us keep on with our play."

Nezahualpilli easily won the next three games. Gloomily, Moctezuma bade farewell to the Texcocan king and shut himself up alone in one of his palaces to brood.

❋ ❋ ❋ ❋ ❋ ❋ ❋ ❋ ❋

CHAPTER 26

The
Comet of 1516

One midnight in the year 1516, the youth who that year had been chosen to represent the Hummingbird, saw from the top of great temple a large comet advancing into the sky like a white giant. He was transfixed, but finally awoke the soldiers of the guard.

"Wake up, sleepyheads! It is not your business to sleep, but to keep awake." His voice trembled with emotion. "Get up and see what comes out of the East—there in the East, like a white cloud."

The soldiers, astonished at the great traveler of the sky, stood entranced until dawn, when the comet was consumed by the rays of the sun.

The young representative of the Hummingbird hurried to inform Moctezuma. He described the apparition, its colossal size, the burning nucleus, the long luminous tail.

The emperor refused to believe. "The chances are you dreamed it all!"

But he passed the day in nervous expectation. When night came, he seated himself on the palace roof. When the comet reappeared, he watched it, breathless with admiration. He called back the youth. "Tell me, young god, what does this sign mean?"

"Oh, Great Majesty, I am a poor ignorant servant, not an astrologer, soothsayer or sorcerer. Call in those who know of nightly things."

Moctezuma called in the astrologers and sorcerers and asked them if they had seen the new sign that had appeared in the sky. None had.

Indignantly the emperor upbraided them. "Is this the sort of watch you keep? Why do I have astrologers and diviners? What good are you?"

He ordered his guards to take the diviners to prison and let them die of hunger.

Once more he sent for the Texcocan king. Nezahualpilli was surprised that Moctezuma had not noticed the comet until now.

"All this portends terrible events for our kingdoms, great catastrophes. Nothing will avert them. There will be innumerable deaths; we are doomed to lose all of our kingdoms. All this will occur in your time."

The emperor began weeping bitterly, like a child. "O gods on high, gods of day and of night and of air, change me into a stick that I shall not suffer, into a stone that I shall not weep, into a bird to fly far from the troubles that await me."

The news of the comet and its meaning traveled to all the provinces of the realm. Every dawn people gathered to watch the comet, and wail and lament. The end of the world was at hand.

CHAPTER 27

Moctezuma's Flight

The emperor continued to be made miserable with evil prophecies. *By 1518, the first bearded white men set foot on Yucatán soil and the rumors of disaster gathered volume.* Believing that he had neither the force nor the courage to combat fate, and that the coming calamities could not be avoided by any human effort, the emperor made up his mind to flee where he would never be heard of again.

He selected the magic cave of Cicalco, House-of-the-Grandmother, between Tenochtitlán and Coyoacán. Some legends said the cave was a place of delight; others, that it was a place of torment and suffering. It was said that Huemac, who long before had ruled Tula, lived there.

The emperor called in his dwarfs and hunchbacks. "Do you wish to go away with me? I shall take you to the Grandmother Cave where we shall find King Huemac. There we shall find eternal life with all the finest comforts. It is well known that King Huemac is the most happy being known."

He sent a message to Huemac to ask whether the ancient king was disposed to receive them. He ordered ten men flayed and called in several soothsayers. "Take these skins and these hunchbacks to the Paradise of Cicalco and give them to King Huemac, saying: 'Moctezuma, your vassal, greets you and desires to enter your service!'"

At the entrance to the cave, the messengers met an aged Negro, Totec Chichahua, leaning on a staff. "Who are you and where are you from?" he asked.

"Sir, we bring a message and gifts from the emperor to King Huemac."

Totec replied, "I shall guide you."

In the presence of powerful Huemac, the guide said: "King and Lord, these boors come from earth, sent by Moctezuma."

"What do these boors want? What does Moctezuma say?"

"Great Lord," replied the ambassadors, "Moctezuma sends you these gifts; he begs to kiss your royal hands and feet; he pleads that you take him into your service, even if only as a sweeper of the palace."

"Return, ask your king what his troubles are, and I will provide the remedy for them." Giving them fruits and flowers, he added: "Return to earth and give him these squashes, these tomatoes, these gourds, these tender corn ears."

Dissatisfied by the report his ambassador brought back, the emperor called in his majordomo. "Take these pigs to the prison to be stoned to death."

He prepared a second expedition, with more human skins and hunchbacks. "Keep all this a profound secret; if you talk, I will throw you alive into a fire, you and your wives and children."

The new ambassadors departed secretly. No Negro was encountered at Cicalco, but an almost blind inhabitant of the subterranean world, with tiny eyes and mouth, small as straws, led them into Huemac's presence.

"Emperor Moctezuma greets you and sends you these presents. He is disturbed by certain prophecies told him by King Nezahualpilli, threatening him with disgrace. He wishes to know what this disgrace may be. He wishes to know the meaning of the serpent cloud which rose up into the night sky. What does it signify? He wishes to enter your service as an humble servant."

Said Huemac: "Moctezuma imagines this world here to be like that in which he now rules, a paradise. In reality, the torments suffered here are eternal. In this place of terror, he will have to take refuge in the center of a rock. May he live and enjoy what he now has, his precious stones, his gold, his rich plumes, his beautiful cloaks, his delicious food and drink. Let him not seek to know more."

This reply irritated the emperor even more and he ordered his majordomo to imprison "these villains and kill them."

He called in two nobles. "In my name, go to Huemac, to the Cave of Cicalco."

If their mission resulted favorably, he said, he would recompense them with gifts and slaves. But if they told anyone of the affair, he would raze their homes and plow up their crops.

The nobles discovered the cave. A guard blocked their path. "Who are you? What do you wish?"

"We have been sent by Moctezuma to King Huemac," they replied.

"I shall conduct you to his presence."

The ambassadors prostrated themselves before Huemac. "Powerful Lord, your vassal Moctezuma sends you these little gifts and begs you to admit him into your empire. He fears the vengeance and disasters menacing him."

"Let him know," replied Huemac, "that he himself has made his ruin inevitable because of the cruel arrogance with which he takes the life of his fellow-beings. Let him do penance, abandon his beautiful robes, his exquisite meals, his roses and perfumes. Let him eat the bread of the poor, drink water cooked with a little bean powder, and be pure. If he obeys I shall show myself on the heights of Grasshopper Hill and will meet him in the island in the middle of the lake."

When Moctezuma heard the nobles' report he was satisfied. He gave them important public posts and gifts of great value.

For eighty days he observed the penitence prescribed by Huemac, divesting himself of every comfort. Believing himself purified, he told the two nobles to return to Cicalco and inform Huemac.

"Very well," replied Huemac, "Tell Moctezuma that within four days I shall show myself on top of Grasshopper Hill. Let him take a canoe and wait for me in the lake."

Moctezuma was jubilant. He heaped gifts on his ambassadors. He gave secret orders to have a small lake island decorated with branches and flowers, and for his slaves, dwarfs, and hunchbacks to keep day and night watch for Huemac's signal. "I am ready to take you to the delectable place I have told you about. Gather many leaves of sapotes, corn and vines, go to the center of the deep lagoon, where you will find a dwelling. Cover the floor with fresh leaves."

At midnight of the fourth day there appeared on Grasshopper Hill a white stone so dazzling it lit up the entire city, the lakes, even the far mountains. Huemac's signal! Watchers raced to tell Moctezuma.

Dressed in state with jewels and valuable feathers, he embarked with his weeping hunchbacks, dwarfs and slaves.

"Do not weep," Moctezuma admonished them, "for we shall live forever in pleasure and happiness, with no memory of our death."

A light lit up the lake, bright as noon. Houses and hills showed up plainly. Huemac was coming toward them.

Near an island was a temple where Tzoncoztl, a high priest and representative of the gods, lived. He was sleeping tranquilly when a mighty voice broke the stillness of night. "Awake, O representative of the gods. Behold, Emperor Moctezuma is fleeing. He goes to the cave of Huemac."

Fully awakened, the high priest heard the same cry: "Moctezuma is fleeing. Huemac awaits him on the lake."

As the bright light shone upon the water, the mighty voice commanded: "Tell him to abandon his attempt to flee to the cave of Huemac. Tell him to return to his palace."

Tzoncoztl jumped into a canoe and, paddling to the island, faced Moctezuma. "What does this mean, most powerful Lord? What scurviness is this in one of so much valor and quality? What will those of Tlaxcala, of Huejotzinco, of Cholula and of Tliliuquitépec; those of Michoacán and Metzitlán and of Yopitzinco say? Where will Mexico be,

Mexico the heart of the whole earth? Will you ruin the empire, which heads the world, merely to satisfy your own whims? It will shame your great city and all who remain in it, if news gets about that you have fled. If you die and they see you die and you are then buried, that is natural. But to flee! What will people say? What shall we say to those, both friends and enemies, who ask for our emperor? Shall we reply with shame that he has fled? That he, who knew how to subjugate sundry and all, up to the confines of heaven itself, now places himself in the basest role of man; throwing away his heritage and that of his descendants. Take courage, my Lord, return to your throne and forget this baseness. Put your cowardly, vain thoughts away. Think of the dishonor you will visit upon all of us."

The priest lifted the plumes from his bowed head in sorrow and humility.

Moctezuma was thoroughly ashamed. Sighing, he looked toward Grasshopper Hill. The light was now extinguished. The world was dark, not a light anywhere. To the priest, the representative of the god, he said, "I beg of you, never disclose this baseness."

Getting into his vessel with all his followers and the priest, he returned quickly to Mexico City. There he shut himself up in his palace. The high priest comforted him constantly, and Moctezuma heaped great honors and riches on him and kept him by his side as his companion.

❋ ❋ ❋ ❋ ❋ ❋ ❋ ❋ ❋

CHAPTER 28

Conquest

With the story of Moctezuma's return to the capital, the legend of the Aztecs, mingling history with magic, comes to an end, and the harsh light of history as we know it illuminates the increasingly tragic story. The hour of disaster was approaching.

Early in 1517 Hernández de Córdoba, captain of three Cuban sailing vessels in quest of Indian slaves, was driven south upon the flat coasts of Yucatán.

Greatly impressed by the Maya civilization, on his return to Cuba he outfitted four vessels for his nephew Juan de Grijalva to explore further. Grijalva sailed along the eastern coast of Mexico as far north as Pánuco, Place of Pulque, and returned to Cuba rich with goods, gold and legends.

The governor of the island, fired by the sight of gold discs, sent out another vessel under the command of Cristóbal de Olid, and authorized a still larger expedition under Hernán Cortés, a Cuban landowner, to follow later.

Cortés spent all his own money, mortgaged his property, borrowed from businessmen and friends and assembled eleven vessels, ten heavy guns, four falconets, much ammunition, sixteen horses, 110 sailors, 553 soldiers and more than two hundred Indians.

Sailing on February 18, 1519, in defiance of the governor's last-minute orders, he went forward on a career that was to take him to lofty Tenochtitlán. He and his followers first landed on the island of Cozumel off Yucatán in the far southeast, where he hurled down the temple idols and erected a Christian sanctuary.

The news of his violences spread fast. People were fired to resistance. In Tabasco his forces were almost overwhelmed by an army that stretched as far as the eye could reach across the broad plains of Ceutla. His flanking cavalry saved the day. The Tabascans, never having seen a horseman, half animal, half beast, fled in terror. The Spaniards mowed them down with great slaughter. All these events were transmitted to Moctezuma by the most accurate picture-writing. The emperor gazed upon the Spanish ships, the strange fire-belching cannon and harquebuses; the men in armor, the strange new man-beast creatures, and he was filled with astonishment, horror and fear. So they were true, the portents of the doom of the empire and his own downfall!

On Good Friday the Spaniards went ashore near what is now Vera Cruz and threw up shelters against the hot sun and tropic storms. They were now on soil over which Moctezuma claimed direct sovereignty. *This occurred in the year One Acatl, or One Reed—the year Quetzalcoatl had promised to return.*

The emperor received prompt tidings of the latest move of the invaders. On Easter Sunday (*the fourth Aztec month of the Long Fast)*, the Aztec chieftain of Vera Cruz appeared to the Spaniards with gifts from the emperor: cloth, gold ornaments, jade and other valuable objects.

Cortés's eyes gleamed. He sent back gifts of beads, bells, mirrors, with a demand for an interview. Among his gifts was a helmet, which the Conquistador asked to be returned filled with gold dust. "We Spaniards," he said, "have a sickness of the heart which can be cured only with gold."

The emperor was more alarmed than ever. He studied the picture-writing his artists had made of the newcomers; their dress, their strange beards, their horses, the charging cavalry, the blasts of the artillery. He was filled with dismay.

Was it possible that the White God, the Plumed Serpent, who had originally vanished across the sea, really had returned to rule over Mexico? Was Cortés really the god returning? If so, it was useless to resist him. *Lately Moctezuma's soothsayers had laid before him still more evil omens: an inexplicable tidal wave on Lake Texcoco, a conflagration, the strange actions of birds—a pheasant with a mirror on its head—a dozen and one evil signs.* His doom seemed inevitable.

Sending more rich gifts to Cortés, he commanded the Spaniards to leave the land in a friendly spirit. Not only did the emperor fill the helmet with pure gold to the brim, but he sent heaps of gold and silver ornaments and precious stones, great sunburst wheels of gold, great moon-burst wheels of silver. Fatal mistake! The Spaniards' greed was fired to fever pitch.

But pestilence had hit Cortes's troops. They were suffering from the heat and the mosquitoes. Many, in spite of their lust for gold, feared they would lose their lives in an assault upon such a mighty empire. Conspiracy was brewing.

Cortés put the ringleaders in irons; the rest he bought off with gold. The nearby powerful Totonaca kingdom offered him an alliance.

Cortés led his forces straight to Cempoalla, the Totonac capital, a white-stucco city of thirty thousand inhabitants. He was received with great courtesy and his little force was assigned to the spacious temple courtyard.

Discovering that some of his followers planned to seize one of the vessels and return to Cuba, the conquistador boldly dismantled all his ships and sank them in the harbor. His men could only go forward—to conquer or to die!

He pushed preparations for the march inland. As a garrison had to be left behind, he was reduced to about four hundred men, fifteen horses and seven pieces of artillery. But he was reinforced by thirteen hundred Totonac warriors and a thousand porters to carry equipment.

The way lay up through the luxuriant foothills, but at the high mountain passes they encountered cold winds and rain—a severe trial after their stay in the hot lowlands. Soon they passed through the massive walls defending the independent Tlaxcalan republic.

Here Cortés had to fight four bitter battles and cut off prisoners' hands and ears before he could make a triumphant entry. He described the city of Tlaxcala as being as large and well built as Granada.

After much feasting his men, reinforced by six thousand Tlaxcalan soldiers, pushed on to Choluda. Here, too, the invaders were warmly welcomed.

But Cortés suspected treachery. Falsely claiming to have discovered a plot, he fell on a public gathering and slaughtered two thousand defenseless men, women and children.

After this dreadful lesson, which was duly reported to the emperor, the Spaniards and their allies moved on toward Tenochtitlán by the most direct route, straight across the high snow saddle between the lofty volcanoes, the two sacred 17,000-foot volcanoes. This was the regular Aztec highway to the coast, and wayside shelters had been built for travelers. Even so, it was difficult getting through the deep snow and over the glaciers. But hardship seemed compensated for when the little army gazed upon the rich, populous Valley of Mexico, with its glistening lakes, its rich gardens, its splendid cities.

Before Cortés entered the Mexican capital, the Lord of Texcoco came out with a load of gold, and told him that Emperor Moctezuma promised still more gold and payment of an annual tribute if the Spaniard would leave his realm. The gifts fired Spanish cupidity to a frenzy.

Cautiously the Spaniards passed along mighty dikes between the lakes to Ixtapalapa and the Hill of the Star to the south of the city. Here they were received cordially by a relative of Moctezuma and quartered in a magnificent palace. The beautiful gardens here, in which the flora of the whole empire was arranged in scientific order, the zoological display, and the aquariums of rare fresh and marine fish, aroused the astonished admiration of the aggressors.

Bernal Díaz was very impressed with their "spacious and well-built lodgings—houses of beautiful stonework and cedar and the wood of the aromatic trees . . . grand rooms and courts, wonderful to behold."

To the Spanish king, Cortés wrote that the buildings of the Salt City were "as large and well constructed, not only in the stonework, but also in the woodwork, and with all arrangements for every kind of household conveniences," as any edifices in Spain. "The temples," he noted, "were carved with figures and the woodwork is all wrought with monsters and other shapes."

The next day, November 18, 1519, they put foot on one of the three main causeways into the city. Its massive masonry astonished them. Great throngs of curious people crowded the banks. A swarm of flower-decked canoes stretched as far as the eye could see.

At the city gate with its tall double towers and crenelated battlements, the Spaniards were greeted by a thousand nobles, all richly dressed. Each in turn, on speaking to Cortés, placed his hand on the ground, then kissed the ground.

"I waited for nearly an hour." Cortés wrote the Spanish king, "while they performed this ceremony."

His cavalry then clattered unopposed across the lowered drawbridge. They were inside the great Aztec capital—and without a blow.

Here, at the head of another large body of nobles, three officers of state advanced, bearing golden wands. Behind in a palanquin blazing with gold, under a canopy glistening with bright feathers, jewels and silver, came Emperor Moctezuma. Uniformed pages swept the roadway and laid down rugs with rich designs when he descended.

The two leaders met near the great aqueduct that supplied the Moyotlán quarter with water and where a few years later, in 1524, the Hospital of Jesús Nazarene was erected—perhaps the first in the New World. *It is still in operation with the endowment bequeathed by the Conquistador, a place of beautiful blue tiles, carvings, statuary and quiet peace.*

Moctezuma stood with great dignity flanked by two nobles. He was clad in a square cloak, richly embroidered; his jeweled sandals had gold soles. From his head circlet floated royal emerald plumes. He was about forty years of age, tall, thin but well built, his hair black and straight, cut fairly short. He had a small, well shaped beard. (Few Indians had hair on their faces.)

Cortés immediately dismounted from his horse. His Indian mistress and interpreter Marina stood at his side. He took off a glass necklace and put it about the neck of Moctezuma. The latter took off his own collar of carved bones and tinted sea shells and put it about Cortés' neck. The Spaniard started to embrace the emperor. The horrified nobles immediately interposed themselves.

With flags flying, music playing, the invaders crossed bridge after bridge over the canals, deep into the heart of the city—larger than any metropolis in Europe. The invaders were awed by the imposing stone buildings, the large squares, the markets and gardens, the lofty pyramid temples. The canals, the streets, the roofs were crowded with tens of thousands of people in bright clothing, a gay and thrilling sight.

At this time the Aztecs commonly wore clothes of brightly dyed cotton, often richly embroidered. The men wore bright richly designed capes, clasped at one shoulder and reaching to cotton trousers, held up by a broad sash, knotted so that triangular points hung before and behind.

The women wore one or more bright sleeveless embroidered or patterned blouses, ankle-length skirts of bright blue and brown, gold scarves and light leather sandals.

Poorer folk, though many also had cotton clothing, often used woven cloth of rougher fibres, from the maguey, palmettos, etc. Richer people also used bird plumage, adorned with gold, on their heads and often down their backs; jeweled necklaces; nose and ear adornments of gold and emeralds. Gold bands often extended from knee to ankles. Perfume was used by both men and women.

At this time the city had 50,000 dwellings in five large barrios, or neighborhoods, each in turn divided into a half a dozen to a score of wards. The main plaza, with its vast teocalli, had 78 temples, the great teocalli, main pyramid. Alongside was the Emperor's vast rose-colored lava palace.

Each quarter of the city had its own separate religious center. The massive teocalli of the Tlaltetoco quarter, a temple called Momoxtli, rose from the great market— larger even than that in the city proper, larger than the whole city of Salamanca in Spain. From 40,000 to 70,000 people came here daily, and the bargaining was so shrill and excited that it could be heard, according to the chronicler Bernal Díaz, three miles away.

The markets were very well ordered, so that each product had its proper locale. A whole street was occupied by herb and medicinal-root vendors and drugstores where processed medicines and salves were sold. There were many barbershops. Clothing, furs, rugs, hangings were sold, and terra-cotta ware, often delicate and thin. Precious stones, gold and silver jewelry were on display. Open-air restaurants, sometimes under palm roofs, served breads, pies, fried fish, stews. There were slave blocks and pens for domestic and wild animals.

Fish, fruits and vegetables were piled high. Inspectors saw that the food was in good condition and that the proper weights and measures were observed. A court of justice for settling any disputes stood near the main entrance.

The Spaniards were assigned to quarters in the palace. Finally, alone with Moctezuma, Cortés addressed him earnestly about the Catholic religion. That alone, he told the emperor, would save his soul and that of his people. The emperor argued that his own gods were also powerful and good.

Despite the fact that he was so kindly received and so lavishly entertained, Cortés soon invented an excuse to seize Moctezuma and clap him in irons in the Spanish quarters. In the courtyard, his soldiers burned officers and chieftains alive over firewood of Aztec javelins. Mass was then said in the great temple of the Aztecs, from which the native gods had been thrown into the square below. The royal treasures were seized and distributed among the soldiers, who fought like snarling curs over the loot.

Cortés was informed by Moctezuma that a new Spanish expedition had arrived off Mexican shores. With only seventy men, he rushed back to the coast, gathering native reinforcements as he went.

The leader of the new expedition, which numbered nine hundred Spaniards and a thousand Indians, was Panfilo Narvaez. After prolonged futile negotiations, Cortés on a stormy night led his tired men across a stream, surprised the newcomers' forces and routed them completely. With promises and threats, Cortés won over the captured soldiers and dismantled Narvaez's ships.

Tidings came of serious trouble back in Mexico City. Cortés had to rush back. He found his forces besieged.

Pedro de Alvarado, left in charge, had ruthlessly slaughtered the celebrants at the great May fiesta, and his soldiers had looted the dead bodies of their gala adornments. The population had risen as one man.

Cortés saved the situation by persuading Moctezuma to pacify his people.

But a worse attack soon came. This time, when Moctezuma stepped out upon a balcony to try to calm the angry multitude, he was jeered and stoned. The magic of his royalty had vanished forever. Shortly after, he died—of a broken heart, people say.

The Spaniards were now completely hemmed in, unable to communicate with the Aztec leaders. All food supplies were cut off. The palace and the city had become a trap.

After repulsing repeated day and night attacks, the Spaniards realized they had to fight their way out or die of hunger and wounds.

All the causeway bridges had been destroyed. They would have to be replaced or the canals be filled in. Six canals had to be crossed on the Tlacopan Causeway to the east. Cortés ordered timbers to be torn from temple walls and fashioned into portable bridges. Every bit of food was saved, every weapon was examined and tested. Litters were made for the wounded.

The Spaniards started out in the dead of night, but at the fourth canal they were discovered by a woman who was getting water. She fled screaming, and the sentinel in the Huitzilopochtli temple began pounding the *huehuetl*, the big war drum. Warriors came on the run and attacked on all sides and from canoes.

Every step the Spaniards took was bitterly contested. Stones, darts, arrows, fire rained down from every roof. Barricades blocked the avenue. Hordes of fighters struck them at the front and rear and on the flanks. At the fifth bridge the Spaniards were badly beaten and many were killed. The survivors finally reached the sixth canal.

At the main moat at the walls of the city, the portable bridge could not be thrown across. The head of the column, blocked by the open moat, was shoved relentlessly forward by the press of the panic-stricken Spaniards behind. Unable to swim in their heavy steel coats of mail, many were drowned. A few cavalrymen, including Cortés, fended off swarms of attackers and successfully swam their horses across. But gradually the moat was filled in by cannon, supplies, treasure and the bodies of men and horses! Over this lugubrious bridge, the surviving forces fought their bloody way.

Pedro de Alvarado, fighting a desperate rearguard action, was unhorsed, bleeding from his wounds. He ran toward the moat, planted a long lance in the lake bottom and vaulted across, an incredible feat. *To this day that part of the causeway, now a modern street, bears the name Alvarado's Jump.*

The broken Spanish forces fled to Tacubaya, where Cortés sat down under a great lightning-splintered *ahuehuetl* tree and wept over the disaster of "The Sad Night." *The tree still stands.*

After a fierce battle in Otumba, the weary, shattered survivors made their way painfully over the mountains to Tlaxcala. There, among friendly allies, Cortés reorganized his forces and replenished his supplies.

He set forth to reconquer Mexico City. His task would not be easy. By then a leader of great spirit, Cuautemotzín, nephew of Moctezuma, had been crowned emperor, and he was determined to drive the Spaniards from the land.

But native disunity played into Cortés' hands. The Lord of Texcoco, though his kingdom was part of the Aztec federation, welcomed Cortés. In that strategic city across the lake, the Conquistador set up headquarters. There he had boats built to storm the city from the lake side. Gradually he captured suburb after suburb, throwing a circle around Tenochtitlán until the city was besieged.

But time and again the Spaniards were hurled back. Then, in one furious fight, the Spaniards had the good luck to capture Emperor Cuatemotzín. Cortés re-entered the city. He had smashed the central authority of the empire for all time. The spirit of the Aztecs was broken.

The Spaniards held Cuatomotzín's feet in the fire to force him to reveal his hidden treasure. "This is scarcely a bed of roses," he remarked quietly and refused to talk. Later they hanged him in the far-off marshes of Tabasco.

The new White God in the Mexican heavens was a jealous god. Quetzalcoatl had fallen. Tezcatlipoca had fallen; Huitzilopochtli, who had come to rule all the earth and the heavens, had fallen.

As time went on, guns, death by fire, the smashing of old temples, and the burning of the holy books worked havoc with Aztec morale. But earnest Christian preachers fol-

lowed in the wake of the slaughter and havoc of the Conquest and gradually the new teachings took root.

And so more and more the old gods, so closely linked with the everyday beliefs and the happiness of the people, receded into the mists of the past. Even so, some have been hidden behind the Christian altars, many have lingered on in the remote countryside and in the hearts of the people. To this day some have not died.

And the fiery poetry and the legends that engendered them, that put prophecy on the lips of the common Mexican, still live on in the lives and hearts of many of the people.

Footnotes

[1] Often spelled Ometecuhtli. The "h" was added later by modern scholars in an effort to indicate more closely the imagined original pronunciation, and has been omitted in this and similar words as it was by many earlier Spanish authorities. Nor is use made in the text of the curious phonetic alphabet developed in the last few years by etymologists to provide a closer approximation to the original sounds. In the case of the Aztecs, it merely adds confusion to confusion, for the modern Aztec pronunciation is not the same as that used five centuries ago; and even in the earlier period, the pronunciation varied widely from place to place, as records from Guadalajara and Mexico City amply demonstrate. The Spanish tongue is itself phonetic, and strange new spellings to indicate at best unverified pronunciations merely confuse all the older accounts. For sounds not in the Spanish language, the Spaniards used various substitute letters such as, for instance, *x* to answer for *sh*. Hence, Mexico was actually *Méshico;* Oaxaca was *Oashaca;* etc.

² Thirteen, connected with the inner rhythm of life itself, enters into practically all time cycles, based upon accurate knowledge of the movements of the moon, sun and the planet Venus.

³ The *Treatise* of the Ramírez Codex describes a wooden idol of the Plumed Serpent: "The face was that of a bird with a beak . . . rows of teeth, of the tongue showing: from the beak to the middle of the face was yellow with a black band that circled from close to the eyes to below the beak.

⁴ The Russians claim to have accomplished this also, according to reports a few years ago.

⁵ Time was divided as follows:

      Day: Tonalli. Belonging-to-the-Sun, *i.e.* to Tonatiu, from the rising and setting of the sun,

DAY   and comprising eight hours, *i.e.* eight ninety-minute periods.

      Night: Of-the-Xiuteucohya, *i.e.* Belonging-to-the-Lords-and-Masters-of-Darkness.

       5-day week

WEEK   9-night week

       13-day week

MONTH 20 days. Cempohualli, known as Metztli (Moon) or Xihuitl (Plant).

YEAR 365 days. 18 months, plus five *nemontemi*, evil or "idle" days.

VENUS YEAR   about 584 days. *Teoxhuitli*, "Year of God."

Thirteen-Month Cycle: *i.e.* 260 days (twenty weeks, thirteen months) known as Tonalamatl. This cycle provided the movable fiestas. Since this cycle counted in the *nemontemi*, or idle days, its holidays fell on no fixed day of the calendar.

Thirteen-Year Cycle: 360 weeks, 234 months, or 4,680 days, plus 13 *nemontemi*, the year-end "idle" days. These thirteen-year cycles were known as Tochitl, Acatl, Tecpatl and Calli, or Rabbit, Reed, Stone and House, after the name of the day that began the first day of the first year.

Fifty-Two-Year Cycle: 1,440 weeks, 936 months, plus 52 *nemontemi*, also 73 *tonalamatl* or religious cycles. It was called Xiumolpilli, Binding-up-of-the-Years, Year Sheaf.

104 Years. Double the preceding. With this cycle the Venus cycle also coincided. It was called Huehueliztli, the Old or Big Century.

260 Years: Twenty thirteen-year cycles.

1,040 Years: Twenty "century"-cycles. It was called Huehuetéotl, "Of-the-Old-Old-God."

[6] This point is now known as San Antonio Abad.

Bibliography

NOTE: *The surviving codices, on which most of these stories are based, are nearly all preserved in European museums. They are listed in George C. Valiant's book.*

BALLOU, MATURIN M. *Aztec Land*. Cambridge: Riverside Press, 1890.

BRENNER, ANITA. *Idols Behind Altars*. New York: Biblo, 1929.

CORNYN, JOHN HUBERT. *The Story of Quetzalcoatl*. Yellow Springs, Ohio: Antioch Press, 1930.

JOYCE, THOMAS A. *Maya and Mexican Art*. London: Studio, 1921.

DÍAZ DEL CATILLO, Bernal. *The True History of the Conquest of New Spain*. London: Hakluyt Society, 1908–16 (5 vols.)

HEWETT, EDGAR L. *Ancient Life in Mexico and Central America*. New York: Tudor Publishing Company, 1943.

Instituto de Antropología e Historia de México. *Twenty Centuries of Mexican Art*. New York: Museum of Modern Art, 1940.

NUTTALL, ZELIA. *The Aztecs and Their Predecessors in the Valley of Mexico*. Philadelphia: Proceedings American Philosophical Society (Vol. 65, pp. 242–255), 1926.

REDFIELD, ROBERT. *Tepoztlán*. Chicago: University of Chicago Press, 1930.

SAVILLE, MARSHALL L. *Woodcarvers Art in Ancient Mexico*. New York: Museum of the American Indian, Heyde Foundation (Vol. 9), 1925.

SPINDEN, HERBERT J. *Ancient Civilizations of Mexico and Central America*. New York: American Museum of Natural History (2nd ed.), 1922.

TOOR, FRANCES. *Mexican Folkways*. New York: Crown Publishers, Inc., 1949.

VALIANT, GEORGE C. *Aztecs of Mexico*. Garden City, New York: Doubleday-Doran, 1941.

VON HAGEN, VICTOR W. *The Aztec Man and Tribe*. New York: New Modern Library, 1958.

Index